Copyright © 2022 by Maddison Cole

All rights reserved. No part of this publication may be reproduced, stored or transmitted in any form or by any means, electronic, mechanical, photocopying, recording, scanning, or otherwise without written permission from the publisher. It is illegal to copy this book, post it to a website, or distribute it by any other means without permission.

This novel is entirely a work of fiction. The names, characters and incidents portrayed in it are the work of the author's imagination. Any resemblance to actual persons, living or dead, events or localities is entirely coincidental.

Maddison Cole asserts the moral right to be identified as the author of this work.

Maddison Cole has no responsibility for the persistence or accuracy of URLs for external or third-party Internet Websites referred to in this publication and does not guarantee that any content on such Websites is, or will remain, accurate or appropriate.

Designations used by companies to distinguish their products are often claimed as trademarks. All brand names and product names used in this book and on its cover are trade names, service marks, trademarks and registered trademarks of their respective owners. The publishers and the book are not associated with any product or vendor mentioned in this book. None of the companies referenced within the book have endorsed the book.

First Edition.

Ebook ISBN: B0B4F8DLTV

Paperback ISBN: 9798837196256

Editing: Emma Luna at Moonlight Author Services

Cover Design: Jessica Mohring at Raven Ink Covers

Formatting: Emma Luna at Moonlight Author Services

DEDICATION

For the fans who, like me, just couldn't get enough Candy in their lives.

AUTHOR NOTE

The writing in this book is the Queen's English, but please don't hold the fact I'm a Brit against me! I can't help it, but I have worked hard to make sure you understand what I am talking about. If anything confuses you, give me a shout!

Please Note - This prequel is based on the thirteen-year-old version of Candy Crystal from my 18+ series, I Love Candy. This feisty FMC is a foul-mouthed, murder-hungry psycho who will leave you in hysterics. This novella, although dark, shows her origins. There's no under age antics mentioned in this book, but that doesn't mean she doesn't make up for it in the main series.

Trigger Warning: The 'I Love Candy Series' features a feisty female lead and her broody harem. Candy is spontaneous, impulsive and reckless, which makes this book inappropriate for under 18's. She gives as good as she gets, causing chaos and usually leaves you wondering who is bullying who! Expect excessive amounts of steam, violence and cursing throughout. This series is a RH trilogy with a HEA…eventually!

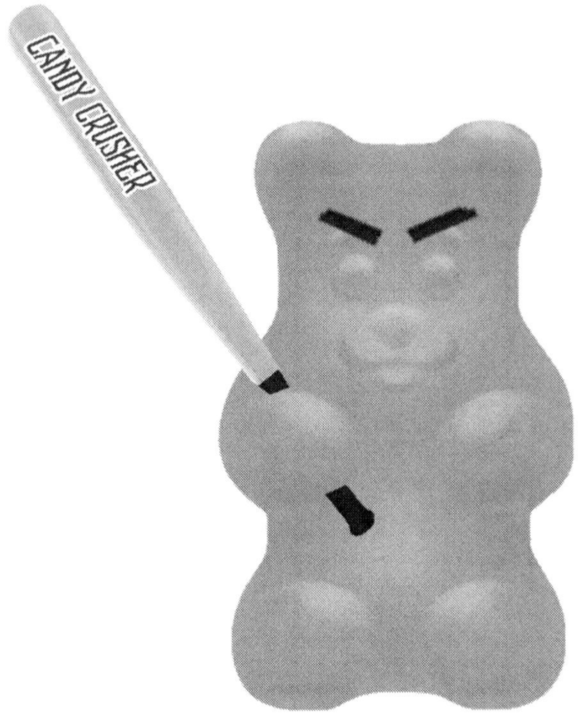
CANDY CRUSHER

Dumpster Chic Is The New Vogue

Run. Just keep never looking back. That's the mantra rolling through my head as my bare feet splash through the black puddles lining the sidewalk. I duck and dodge between the queues waiting around the block in the hopes of being permitted entry to some seedy club or another. High heels click loudly, the party-goers not deterred by a recent downfall. Hands reach out, trying to grab my slender thirteen year-old frame. The hospital gown hiding my lanky frame slips through their fingers, whipping wildly as I make my escape. Their alarmed calls chase behind me, whilst I'm hunting for somewhere out of sight to catch my breath.

An alleyway presents itself as my salvation and I duck inside, doubling over as my body finally gives in to the tremors. Scrunching my eyes shut, I try to piece together my erratic thoughts. Try to find the truth amongst my fears. If there was something I missed, some sign I didn't need to jump out of the window and become a runaway, I can't find it. It was the last doctor that tipped the scales. That last lingering look of 'you deserved this'.

I rub my torso uncomfortably, still feeling their gloved hands inspecting the mass of bruises coating my frail skin. And if I allow my mind to travel any deeper, I can almost imagine my foster father and his friends pinning me down. Their steel grip on my wrists, my ankles, my throat. I heave, not having anything to throw up, but a state of nausea grips me anyway. A cackle rolls from someone passing the end of the alley and I jolt back into action, using a dumpster lid to hoist myself over a barbed fence. The spikes catch my thighs, tearing splits through the purple stains already marring my body, but it doesn't matter anyway. Nothing matters, except that I'm alive. Alive and alone.

Landing heavily on the other side of the fence, I take off the network of back streets that hide in the city's shadow. Away from civilization, where the strays hiss and the vermin bite.

My English teacher always said I had a knack for spinning a story, and that's what the police said too. My gut drops as it suddenly dawns on me, in the light of recent events, I won't be returning to Creston High. It's a stupid thing to get upset about, all things considered, but it's the one thing that hits me the hardest. I wasn't popular by any means. I was that quiet kid at the back of the class, with a book in hand and torn clothing. The one that those with perfect, married parents would snigger at. The one who looked forward to her free lunch, since it was sometimes the only meal she'd get, thanks to a lousy foster mom and up to eight other unwanted brats. Still, the school had a roof, a library, and teachers I thought cared.

Hanging my head low, I misjudge my step, stumbling off the pavement and directly into the glare of an oncoming vehicle. This is it, I think. The horn blares and I stand stock still, ready for that to be the last sound I hear. The one that I hope knocks me into some sort of afterlife where I might actually find solace.

A strong arm curls around my midsection, jarring me from my peaceful reprieve, and whips me aside as the car whizzes past.

"Not yet," a strong voice tells me, walking me back towards the alley I just ran from. "You've got a lot more to give, little one. I can tell."

He pats my head, giving my overgrown, brunette hair a small shake. My mind races, struggling to comprehend what just happened. Was I really ready to die, and why did this man save me? But the heat flaring at my back reminds me he's still loosely holding me, so I jerk away from his touch. He chuckles, unfazed by the murderous glare I try to give. It falls flat when I get my first real look at his face, framed by the glow of a street lamp.

He's younger than I expected, maybe in his twenties. His layered clothes are torn in various places, and dirt cakes most of the others. Fingerless gloves frail around his knuckles, as does the beanie pulled over his tatty, dark hair. It's his shoes that grab my attention the most though; a pair of polished, black biker boots, shining proudly without a spec of dirt on them.

"You like?" he asks, following my eye line. I drop my gaze to my wiggling toes, all too aware of the numbness claiming the soles of my feet, and I nod. "I'll show you how to get a pair of your own, if you like." My brows lift and the small smile feels foreign on my face. He jerks his chin, turning his back, and I'm eager to follow. The various coats hanging from his shoulders stop at different lengths, the longest underneath reaching the back of his knees. It's clear he knows these streets, it's evident in the confidence of his strides.

We turn so many corners. I wouldn't even be able to find my way back with a map, yet something tells me wherever we're going, I'll not be returning. Not as the vulnerable girl that went in, at least.

"Let me guess, orphanage kid?" the man muses, almost to himself, but I answer anyway.

"How did you know?"

"Most of the runaways are." With a knowing look that puts me at ease, he pauses by what I think is a storage container, but as he props open the rusted door, I see it's so much more. An entire village in the form of a flea market is visible inside, the storage units all interlinking to create a lengthy, sheltered space. Other units branch off into thin hallways covered by velvet curtains. Some of the women waiting outside, in not much more than a bikini and heels, allude to what happens behind those curtains, and it's not a place I'll be eager to visit.

"Shall we?" the man asks, holding out his arm. I gingerly take it, still very aware that I'm freezing beneath the paper-thin hospital gown that has some men already leering.

Recoiling behind the man's six-foot frame, he shifts to hold open his many jackets and gently eases me inside. I huddle against his body, too thankful for the concealment to worry about being this close to an older man's body again so soon. I don't think it's a feeling I'll ever grow accustomed to. But, with each of his gentle steps keeping in time with my awkward shuffles, I start to thaw.

Together, we shift through the crowd while I peer out, fascinated by the exchanges happening all around. Thrift stalls stand shoulder to shoulder, all selling a different variation of the same items. Some clothing, some jewellery, stationary and knickknacks, cardboard boxes of food and drinks. Yet they're not selling these random items, instead they're trading them amongst themselves.

A gypsy woman, covered in clinking pendants along her headscarf, swaps a bottle of wine for a hamper of tins and vegetables. Several children pop out from beneath her stall, taking the hamper in their greedy hands and scampering off out of sight. Another pair on the opposite side are bartering to see how many fillets of fish a thick, padded jacket that could double as a sleeping bag is worth.

"So, what do they call you?" His voice makes me jump. The question rumbles through my side, reminding me how closely I'm huddled to this stranger.

"Oh, um. Candi—" The argument about the jacket picks up, and one of the men is shoved into us. I take most of the hit, knocking me into the stranger's sharp ribs. Contrary to his bulky appearance, I reckon the man hiding inside these layers is almost as skinny as me. No, not skinny—underfed. Coming to my defence once again, his arm crowds around me protectively as he curses loudly and steers me away.

"Watch it, will ya! Carrying precious cargo here!" he cries out and I balk. The other men still at the voice, instantly bowing their heads and retreating.

"Sorry, Patrick. Didn't realize it was you."

"Won't happen again," they mutter, retreating back behind their stalls. In fact, many heads have peaked up to get an eyeful of me peering out of Patrick's jacket.

"It's a violent world," he chuckles, once we're safely out of the main market area. "But you must know all about that. Am I right, Candy?"

I blink a few times, noting the nickname he gives me. Or I unknowingly gave myself. But, why not? This is my reinvention. I can be whoever I want to be. So, from this day forth, I'll be

Candy. Candy…I look around, spying an obviously fake diamond, set into a rusting gold necklace on the nearest stall. It's perfect. A smile warms my cheeks, the start of a reinvention simmering through me. I'm Candy Crystal, and from now on, nothing is going to hold me back.

It Takes A Bitch To Train A Pup

"The trick is to start small. See what you want, and wait for the perfect opportunity to take it." Patrick kneels down, pulling me into a crouch by his side. We peer at a news stand on the corner, concealed by the cover of a parked car. Morning has just broken, the sky begins to lighten as the woman receives her first delivery. A stack of papers tied in string, which she turns her attention to setting out. "This is it, get ready," my savior tells me.

I scratch at the label, tugging on the back of my neck, nerves wriggling around in my gut. Patrick doesn't need to pick pockets or steal in the ways he's been describing to me. He walks up to various market stalls in the storage village and plucks out whatever he wants. No one dared to question him, especially when he held their gazes so confidently, they merely turned away. Apparently, on this occasion, what he wanted was an itchy jumper made from synthetic wool, and a pair of baggy cargos for me to wear. Still, even as I sneak forward with the excess of material fisted in my hands, it's better than being naked under the hospital gown. No shoes yet, though.

Creeping up behind me, Patrick's heated breath warms my ear. "You see something you want?" he asks huskily. I catch his eye, confused by the humor in their muddy brown depths. Frowning, I concentrate on the news stand. Scanning the products covering the stand, I nod, confirming my decision.

"Then go get it." Patrick chuckles.

Exhaling, I wait for the woman to turn the opposite way before I dash forward. There's no cars around to obstruct my way, nor are there any other people to witness what I'm about to do. My feet burn from the many lacerations lining my soles, ones that will no doubt be infected by the dirty road pressing against each cut.

Reaching the corner of the stand, I duck down, remaining out of view for a few more precious seconds. Tingles crawl down my arm, numbing my fingers until I'm not sure if they'll work properly. But, after counting myself down from three, I dart around the stand, clasping a packet of bubblegum in my grip as a dog lunges forward. His chain yanks him back from sinking his bared teeth in my face, his echoing bark blaring through the empty street like a siren.

"Oi! Thief!" The newsstand woman whips around, diving over the counter to grab my wrist. I shriek and fight against her hold, searching desperately for any hint of Patrick. He's nowhere to be seen. Releasing the gum, I buck and twist enough for my skinny wrist to pry free, and then bolt down the street without looking back.

Hands fisted in the baggy cargos, I don't stop until the houses spread out enough for a playground to become visible. I'm not in the mood to play, but the concealed tunnel in the center of the climbing frame beckons me forward. The gate squeaks noisily and the bark-layered ground adds more cuts to my aching feet.

Dragging myself up the rope ladder, I flop into the tunnel, a mess of ragged breathing and sweat-slickened hair. Once the silence of my oasis settles the pounding of my heart, my body gives in to the nerves I've been holding at bay. Shivers as violent as the kind of tremors you'd have during a seizure rack my frail body, and force the tears to fall from my chocolate brown eyes. This is all I'm destined to be. A failed pickpocket that has no home to hide in and no one to comfort her. Curling up on my side, I let the darkness of my exhaustion take over, with one resounding thought bouncing around my mind. Patrick set me up.

A faint pattering on the edge of my subconscious steadily increases as the thunderous hum of rain smacks the plastic tubing surrounding me. I try to block it out, but the louder it grows, the more I shiver in the itchy jumper that's doing nothing to warm me. My senses arise until I can't even grasp a tendril of the dream that drew me into a false sense of security. Just when I think I can remember it, a wholesome scent enters my system. I grip onto it, inhaling deeply. Salty sweetness and homely warmth, that's how I'd describe it.

Cracking an eye, I rise up onto my knees and flinch at the sight of Patrick crammed into the tunnel beside me. His legs are bent and his neck bowed at an awkward angle, requiring a rub from his fingerless-gloved hand.

My wave of fury is dulled by the open box of fresh waffles in his lap, layered up with rashes of bacon and thick streams of syrup. Drool puddles around my tongue, my teeth creating a wall to keep it from rolling straight out of my mouth. I want to be mad, if the ache in my stomach will let me.

Without saying a word, Patrick moves the box onto my knees and hands me a wooden fork. Sold.

"Take it easy," Patrick chuckles under his breath. "You'll give yourself a stitch eating that fast." I ignore him, barely chewing in favour of getting the food down my throat as quickly as possible. Even before I came to be in the hospital, none of my foster homes ever gave me food like this. I seemed to have a mark on my profile that automatically dumped me into the worst excuses of childcare they had available.

Polishing off the waffles, I toss the box aside and groan as a new type of stomach ache churns within. Covering my middle with crossed arms, I sit as straight as possible, not letting on to Patrick he was right.

"You left me." My voice comes out small. I cringe at my own pathetic-ness, wanting to scrape what's left of my dignity off the floor and leave for good. If only Patrick wasn't the only person alive who has bothered to seek me out.

"I never left," he confesses, in a gravelled voice that sounds older than his years. "I was watching the whole time. Then I got breakfast and followed you here." Dragging the tattered beanie from his head, a mess of dark curls stick out in all directions around his face. The stubble on his jaw looks irritable, judging by the redness underneath, from where Patrick must have recently itched it. His blue eyes are dull, their vibrancy sullied by the life no one should have to live. I can tell Patrick has seen things of nightmares, and as much as I'm furious that he ditched me, I can't help but pity him. After all, I'm in the same boat.

"Don't look at me like that." Patrick ducks his head,

misreading my thoughtful expression. "Failure is part of your training."

"What am I being trained for?" I ask, finally able to straighten as my stomach ache lessens. Swinging his gaze to mine, Patrick's features harden with a sharp nod.

"Survival." We wait out the worst of the rain inside our cramped canopy, re-emerging once frostbite for my bare toes is no longer an added worry. The sun breaks free of the clouds just long enough to give me the illusion a warm summer is on the way, although it always seems to be stormy, wherever I'm concerned.

Keeping my head ducked low, my eyes are trained on Patrick's pristine biker boots as I follow him step for step from the playground. He's careful to avoid muddy patches and puddles, quickly making his way back to a sidewalk where the concrete is much more forgiving. For him, at least. The roughness makes me wince with every step.

Trying to distract myself, I drag shivering fingers through my waist-length hair, fighting against the knots that are permanently located there. The distraction works because by the time I give up on my detangling mission, Patrick halts and I slam into his back. Peering at our surroundings, my heart sinks to see the same newsstand dead ahead.

"Why are we back here?!" I demand, finding some of the fight I was so easily able to give my foster father.

"Rule number one, never give up. This stall is your first assignment, we're not moving on until it has been completed."

"But...you saw. I can't do it," I whine. "There's so many more people around now, and that stupid dog will sense me a mile off."

"Where you find problems, I hear solutions." Patrick steps aside and grips my upper arms to hold me in place. Lowering his head to my height, he looks straight ahead, forcing me to do the same. "Pedestrians give you more cover, and as for the dog, knowing your foe is essential. You've done half the leg work by assessing the stall owner's strengths, now just find a way around them." I have a feeling we're not talking about just the stall anymore, but instead of trying to back out, I put my brain to better use. Maybe slipping through the crowd will work to my advantage, but the dog? I can't see any bones or cats around. Sighing, I drop my head back, ignoring the glare Patrick shoots at the side of my head.

"Why here? Wouldn't a busy store be easier?"

"No surveillance cams, no security," he grumbles impatiently, dropping his hands from my arms. I miss the warmth, but for one reason alone, I'm absolutely freezing. "Look, time is money around here. If you can't master a corner stall, then you don't have the potential I thought you did." My eyes flick up to the blue ones staring back lazily, a lump lodged in my throat.

"And if it turns out I can't do it?" I ask, needing confirmation of what I already know.

"Then I'm done wasting my time on you." Patrick's voice is cold and hard, but it's the motivation I need. Balling my fists, I shift my gaze back onto the stall with renewed focus.

A kid around my age exits a shiny, new-plate car across the street, shouldering a sports bag. A hood frames his face, allowing for the styled curls of sandy-colored hair to poke out. Not dissimilar to Patrick's curls, but this boy's look is intentional, and the lack of sleeves on his jacket tells me his hoodie is for fashion, not function.

Moving to stand by a lamp post, I watch the boy look both ways before crossing the road to head my way. Batting away any last minute nerves, I breathe deeply, more than aware of Patrick watching my every move. Lowering my head, I wait for the boy's fancy high-tops to come into view before barging my way forward, catching his shoulder. The sports bag is knocked to the floor, which I not-so accidently kick away into the closest alleyway.

"Oh God, I'm so sorry." I crouch down, keeping my back to the boy as he fumbles to get around me. Fishing his bag up by the strap, I spin to find him too close and fake a smile. "I need to pay better attention." His large hazel eyes catch me off guard, the fresh scent of his body wash and general cleanliness intoxicates my mind. A blush creeps up my cheeks and I hastily push the strap into his hands, balking that his fingers brush against mine.

"Erm, no problem." He smiles and I melt a little inside. If a boy band member were to jump out of a magazine and flash a line of perfectly straight, pearly whites at me, this is exactly what he'd look like. Doing an awkward curtsey thing, I duck out of his body and walk backwards, giving a little wave. Then I curse myself for being an idiot and spin, heading directly towards the stall. "And thanks, by the way!" his voice calls after me and I shudder.

Focus, Candy, you giddy, stupid plum.

Weaving through passers-by, I get a grip on myself by looking down at the tennis ball clutched in my palm. I may not be a master pickpocket yet, but I've lived with enough foster brothers to learn the art of distraction. This time, I round the opposite side of the stall first, spying the dog lying across a skinny opening in the structure. A wooden countertop has been flipped over to bar entry to the general public, trapping the owner inside and effectively creating a rain cover for the St Bernard underneath. He's as big as I thought, with just as much drool, and his bottom set of teeth stick out over his snout.

Spotting me, his head perks up and a growl resounds through his thickly furred chest. Dodging the owner's cycling, I roll the tennis ball across the ground and directly into the beast's mouth. He accepts it, seeming pleased with his new toy as I lower down and reach out a shaky hand. Closing my eyes, I hold my breath until the softness of his fur greets my palm. His huge head nudges me, demanding I make a proper fuss of him, allowing my chest to finally expand with relief. Part one down.

Leaving my new friend to slobber over his ball, my feet carry me towards the front of the stall where all the sweets sit in beautifully organized rows. The bright colours and shiny packets distract me, but it's the gum I came for and that's the prize I want. Taking a step closer, the owner finishes her current transaction and turns to face me. Tilting her head to the side, the smile drops from her aged face.

"Hey, aren't you..." Her beady eyes narrow on me and I freeze. Just then, a man reaches over me to grab for a paper, and I spot Patrick in a gap between two vehicles over the road. He nods at me expectantly and I bite my bottom lip. Despite knowing he didn't abandon me last time, seeing him now boosts me and reminds me of his advice. Use the surroundings to my advantage. Got it.

"Ew!" I gasp, jerking away from the man reaching for his paper. "Did you just put your hand up my sweater?!" Shocked mutters sound from all of those who have stopped around us, closing in to find out what happened. Spinning and putting my back to the stall, I cross my arms over my chest and hold his gaze. "You did! You totally just tried to grab for my under-developed fried egg breasts!"

The suited man balks, all of the colour draining from his face and a string of stutters leave his lips. Raising his hands in a peaceful gesture, I fake a flinch, twisting towards the display and grabbing the packet of gum in one swift move. Concealing it within my folded arms, I slip through those trying to comfort me and make a run for it. Patrick has disappeared, but I don't panic this time. I find him a few alleyways over, a slow clap reverberating from his palms when he spots my approach.

"Well done, little one. That was much better than I expected," he praises, and I grin until my cheeks hurt. I did it. I did something beneficial to my survival, all by myself. Well, bar a lightly veiled threat by Patrick to leave me behind.

"What did you expect?" I joke, peeling the wrapping from the top of the packet. A car drives past the end of the alley, directly through a puddle that splashes against my back. Luckily, nothing can bring me down from my high right now.

"That you'd be sitting in a jail cell tonight, and I'd never see you again." Patrick shrugs and my smile falters. His blue eyes crinkle at the corners slightly and I relax, starting to get used to his humor. I take a stick of gum from my well-deserved pack when Patrick's fingerless gloves pluck the rest from me, announcing that I've just been 'taxed'.

"Hey! I earnt that!" I grab for the pack. Patrick holds it way out of my reach, using his full six-foot frame to his advantage. Not even my springy jumps put me anywhere near my prize. Grinning, Patrick turns his back on me and I scowl, shoving the one remaining stick in my mouth before he takes that one too.

"Rule number two," he calls back, expecting me to follow. "You're never at the top of the pecking order."

A Witch, A Pirate, and G.I Joe Walk Into A Bar...

Without any other option, I follow Patrick around like a lost puppy hoping for scraps. Equally, as if this morning's lesson was the extent of his duties to me today, he completely ignores me. Picking up envelopes, dropping off packages, dealing in trading, and navigating from one homeless dealer to the next. All the while, he treats me like a ghost. Instead of letting it bother me, I try to piece together the maze of shortcuts and hidden escape routes he leads me through, hoping I can use this city as my playground, when I eventually break away from him. Holes in fences behind dumpsters, locks that are easy to pick, chains we can duck beneath. I learn by observing, barely seeing Patrick's arms twitch as he pickpockets the general public.

With the business crowd beginning to leave their offices, we head into the subway, hunting for the most popular platforms. Curious eyes give us a wide berth, instantly judging Patrick's layers of coats and my blistered, bare feet. They have every right too. Patrick waits for the train to pull up before swooping into the hordes, trying to jump onboard before the doors shut. At the last moment, Patrick's hand whips out to grab my collar and yank me inside.

"Take a load off," he orders, pushing me into a seat before a man in a suit tries to swoop in. Tucking my feet beneath my butt, I pull my hair over the itchy jumper, trying to hide within my fringe. Unlike trailing around the city, the lights inside the train are much brighter, pinning me beneath a stationary spotlight for others to take a good, long look. A girl around my age sits opposite, a little further down the carriage, tucked beneath her mother's arm. They talk of a Broadway show they're on their way to see, thrumming with excitement.

The girl's eyes slide my way, her freckled face offering me a small smile and I scowl back. Don't patronize me with your sympathy when we are living at literally different ends of the spectrum.

Barrelling onwards, Patrick relaxes against a cushioned barrier, an air of superiority about him. He doesn't shy away from the stares, he welcomes them. As if we have every right to be here, despite the lack of a ticket. On his command, I'm drawn from one train to the next, losing any recon I'd managed to gain. By the time we resurface from the subways, Patrick is significantly richer, and I'm thoroughly lost. Evening has set and the familiar gnawing of my stomach arises with the scents wrapping around me.

We've popped up in a central square, brimming with billboards and fast food chains. The traffic is gridlocked, a concoction of blaring horns and angry drivers trying to go home. Rats scurry along the edge of the road, ducking into the sewers, much like how Patrick and I ventured into the subway. I don't have time to pause on that thought, the streams of people shoving me along from my rooted spot. At least the ground has dried, leaving me with only the coldness of the concrete against my bare feet to worry about.

Without pausing, Patrick strides away, leaving me lost as he shifts out of sight. Darting after his jacket tail, the frayed end flipping around the back of his calves, I manage to grab a hold like a baby elephant following its only companion. He doesn't seem to notice, or I'm sure he'd shove me off.

Veering into what appears to be an alleyway from the outside, the dead end rounds out into an elongated oval. Sheets upon sheets of tarpaulin have been tied between the back fence and the surrounding buildings, overlapping like one huge tent. The sections are divided by shopping carts filled with hordes of junk and cardboard signs asking for money. Yet the people sitting around a portable heater are nothing but joyous.

"Patty! Long time no see!" A man who I'm sure is a stranded pirate, who's lost his map to the sea, approaches. A long grey beard falls from his chin, a bandana covering whatever hair he has on his head, and a wooden leg protruding from his stained beach shorts. Gaining the attention of the others, the crowd halt their jokey chatter to jump up and welcome Patrick back. I step into his back, using his bulky clothes to shield me from their crooked, yellow teeth and staggering footsteps. I imagine sleeping on the ground plays hell with one's back, and I decide here and now, I'm getting myself a bed, even if it kills me. It'd be a better fate than winding up hunched over like a lycan in mid-shift.

A woman peers around Patrick's side, a crazed look in her blood-stained eyes, and her bones protruding in all the wrong places.

"What have you brought, Patty?" She smiles a crooked grin, trying to coax me out with her knobbly finger. I scowl, lifting my head and refusing to be referred to as a 'what'. Even if I am shit scared I'm looking into my future reflection.

"I'm Candy," I state boldly, stepping out of Patrick's shadow. He winks down at me, seeming much older than his twenty years.

"Candy's going to be my protégé." He pulls me under his arm. I swallow the panic that rises, accepting his compliment with a wash of pride. "You'd all better watch out. She'll be running these streets before long."

"I'll make a note to stay on your good side then, young Candy. With a teacher like Patty here, I expect you'll out rank him in no time," the pirate tells me. He and Patrick share a laugh while I absorb the words, not realizing there's a pecking order. Obviously Patrick is above me in the sense he is older, but what I'm hearing sounds like he has far more control over everyone than being just some homeless brute.

Now the introductions are over, people move back to crowding around the heater. The hunchback witch waves me over to sit on her dirty blanket, and with the frostbite clawing at my toes, I don't have the stubbornness to deny her invitation.

"You made it just in time," she tells me with a smile. An elderly man with the tattoos of an ex-military soldier pulls out his ukulele and begins to play an upbeat tune everyone can move to. Heads bob, bodies sway, and smiles run free. On second thoughts, maybe the biggest lesson I'll learn today is not to judge so quickly. I am a child of the street now after all, and so far, these are the only people who have ever accepted me with open arms. I wait for the questions to start, already prepping my vague answer, but they never come. Out here, back stories don't matter.

Out of the corner of my eye, Patrick is drawn into conversation with a man who doesn't seem to belong in this setting. Tamed hair falls to his shoulders above a smart, tweed jacket. His long legs are encased in dark slacks, and snuggly on his feet are a pair of shiny dress shoes. I've never been a girly girl who is interested in shoes, but they're quickly becoming my new obsession. Not in a *'I would look sexy in those'* kind of way, but in the obsessive, *'gonna shank someone to cover my feet'* kind of way. At least I'm not alone here with my toes wiggling freely, and even those who do have the luxury of shoes are in desperate need of a fair bit of repair.

My eyes track Patrick handing the man a suspicious envelope from the inside of his many jackets, as headlights turn into the alleyway. I shield my eyes against the brightness, spotting that it's some kind of small van through my fingertips. My hackles immediately rise as the van stops in front of our only escape, but the others around me jump with excited murmurs and so I follow suit. Two women slide out of the cab and head around back to throw the rear van doors open. Getting caught up in the crowd, a hand closes around the back of my sweater and hauls me back a step.

"Hey," the man beside Patrick says, his hand fisted by my nape. "Don't I know you?" Frowning, I scramble in his hold until he releases me. Then I shrug my sweater back into place before replying.

"Me?" I shake my head in confusion. "Nah, I'm nobody." The longer the man stares his shadowed eyes down at me, the more I try to rack my brain for a hint of recognition. It's possible he could have been one of my old foster dad's friends, but not one that visited often. I've committed those faces to memory, waiting for the day I find them again as an adult and make them pay for everything they took from me.

"Mmmmm." He finally presses his lips together. "I wouldn't be so sure." Turning his back and dismissing me, the man returns to his chat with Patrick while I go to see what the commotion is all about at the back of the van. Rounding the royal blue paintwork, my eyes bulge at the fully equipped kitchen set up back here beneath an internal spotlight.

A counter folds out on a kickstand, complete with a gas hob and chopping board area. Further back, a pristine coffee machine shines beside a wall of hanging utensils. The younger of the two women reaches back to pull out a wok, and a shopping bag primed with ingredients. She sets about preparing and cooking a meal, while the other woman, a blonde compared to the other's brunette locks, finishes handing out coffees.

"Hey, sweet thing." She spots me and smiles. The unhindered joy in her face reaches all the way to her pale blue eyes, and when she reaches out to rub my shoulders, I don't shy away. "Haven't seen you before. How about some hot cocoa while we wait for the stir-fry to cook?"

"Oh, yes please," I sigh, finding a warm disposable cup in my hand a moment later. I gulp it down, despite the burning shock to my tongue. It's just right, not too sweet or bitter, and after a few moments, I'm able to slow down to steady sips.

The brunette is stirring a mass of noodles in the giant wok, while her friend attends to chopping long baguettes into slices. In almost no time at all, they announce the food is ready and begin to serve in paper bowls. I brace myself for the stampede that never comes. Instead, everyone fashions themselves into an orderly line that the witch—I mean, vertically challenged woman draws me into. That's when it dawns on me once and for all; this isn't just a group, it's a community. There's a level of respect here I know in my gut is a rare find.

Scents I can't place wrap around me like an embrace until I'm at the front of the line and accepting my bowl. Packed with colour, the green veggies and red peppers are evenly proportioned with the garlic prawns sitting on top, and now my stomach really groans. Throwing my cup in the trash bag provided, I take a wooden fork and move back towards the heater.

"Do they come every night?" I ask a man whose skin is as ghostly white as his hair. He gives a slight shake of his head while wolfing down his meal.

"Only on Tuesdays and Thursdays," he says around a mouthful. "They belong to the Street Angels charity, they own the hostel down the road."

"If there's a hostel down the road, why do you sleep out here?" I ask, too curious not to pry. A dwarf with a full beard sits beside me, offering up a piece of bread I forgot to grab.

"We'd have to queue outside for hours before they begin accepting guests, and even then it's women and children first. You might be able to get a bed most nights, but we prefer to know we have a permanent place to stay." He shrugs, crossing his tiny legs.

"Well, permanent until the state decides we're in their way for some new building complex and shifts us along," the military guy pitches in when he re-joins us.

"And when that happens, we will do as we always do. We pack up and move on," the woman who has taken a liking to me responds.

We fall back into our comfortable silence as we eat, my mind reeling with so many aspects of this lifestyle I didn't know about yesterday. Mostly everyone is back from the meals-on-wheels and the sounds of clattering leads me to believe the women are clearing up.

I look around, finding Patrick has disappeared and my gut churns. Has he left me? Do I even care? I could easily see myself slotting in here, but there's something about the life Patrick leads that intrigues me. He moves wherever he pleases, and anyone who knows of him stays the hell out of the way. There's something to be said for that level of respect. But all of that aside—he called me his protégé. For the first time in my shambles of a life, I mean something to someone. And that seems too good to pass up for twice weekly hot meals and a cardboard bed beneath a sheet of tarp.

As if conjured by my sheer will to see him, Patrick appears from around the van, his dark eyes instantly falling on me. He's carrying two paper bags in his hands, that look like they're on the brink of ripping through. The charity women also appear with matching bags and proceed to hand out bottles of water and packs of cereal bars to each of us. With kind words about meeting my acquaintance, they hop back into their van and reverse out of the alleyway.

"You ready to go kid?" Patrick asks me, and I don't let the pet name dampen my spirits. Considering how today started, this has been a much more optimistic evening. So, when he outstretches his hand, I take it. Saluting everyone goodbye, Patrick leads me away, and I don't even care where we're going.

"How do you know all of those people?" I ask instead, smiling back at those still waving to me.

"Best way for people to have your back is to look out for them. It's a rough world, us vagrants need to stick together." To prove his point, Patrick's arm flies out to stop me from stepping into the road when a car swerves, taking his turn a few seconds too late.

"Vagrants?" I ask, rearranging my skewered sweater. Patrick's eyes linger a moment too long on my non-existent chest, but when I look again, his eyes are glued to the rat running into a drain by my feet.

"Yeah, a person who drifts from place to place, doing what

they have to, in order to survive. You're on the right track to becoming one too." Patrick scruffs up the hair on the top of my head and I grin ear to ear. My chest brims with pride that finally, after bouncing from group home to group home, to being abandoned, I may have found my place to belong at last.

Heterosexual Camping Is Just Sleeping On The Ground

My eyebrows shoot up as we emerge from the subway in a much more affluent area. Rich enough that every street light is shining brightly, and there's not a lick of spray paint in sight. The houses stand tall, coated in sheets of white wash with symmetrical windows splayed across the entire street front. My feet drag as I slump behind Patrick, having fallen asleep on the last train ride. I have no clue where I am, and right now, I don't care. Grabbing hold of an iron railing protecting a small flower patch, Patrick smirks at me over his shoulder.

"Nearly there, kid. Just around the next corner." I've lost all faith in his words since he told me that same thing in the last district. Guess what was around the next corner—a subway station.

Yawning widely, my mind drifts to the sleep I could have had if I'd stayed with the pirate, witch, ghost, dwarf and ex-G.I Joe. Maybe we'd all have huddled up in a slumber pile, comfy and close enough to let the fleas travel from one of us to the next. Rounding the corner Patrick promised is the last, I bump into his body and jump back a step.

"Shit, sorry," I curse and then blush. It's stupid since my foster dad said much worse. Especially when he was whispering disgusting things in my ear while I pretended everything was okay for the social workers, but I never want to turn out like him. The polar opposite would be a clean cut, successful businesswoman who saved orphans in her spare time, but that's not looking likely. I doubt I'll be able to get a stray cat to like me long enough to stick around at this rate.

"Here, I'll give you a boost," Patrick tells me, bracing his hands together. I frown, looking up to where the ladder halts above me, just out of reach. The metal fire escape matches one on the other side of the alley I've found myself in, along with a pair of dumpsters that don't smell like death.

Bracing my hand on the wall, I place an icy foot in Patrick's hand, and he all but throws me up into the air. On a scream, my fingers latch onto the last rung, and thanks to my weight, it shoots down towards the ground. Releasing it just in time, I fall back on my ass with a sharp jolt.

Instead of helping me up, Patrick laughs and ascends the ladder with me scowling up at him from the ground. Pushing myself upright, I climb the ladder with heavy footsteps, causing the rattling metal to ring out as I scale the building. Breaching the top, all arguments die on my tongue at the sight before me.

A mass of tents have been erected, all facing the centre of a circular area where a stack of firewood sits. Solar-powered lights flicker on under the brightness of the moon, deciding it is night time after all. In each tent, various items are stashed away in shoe boxes or duffle bags, all owned by Patrick, if I were to guess. I doubt he's one to share well with others and this type of living arrangement suits him. A castle made of cloth and tarpaulin, as well as a storage facility for all of his stolen goods.

"Welcome to my humble abode." Patrick gestures with a fingerless gloved-hand. He heads for the pile of logs and sets about sparking up a campfire while I stare at the teepee-style tent in the centre of the rooftop. Overhead, the lack of artificial lighting allows for a sky of stars and the glowing full moon to beam back at me.

"Wow," I breathe, finally stepping onto the roof. "This is where you live?" A grunt leaves Patrick as he sparks up a small flame and leans over to blow on it carefully.

"I live wherever I please. I don't choose this life to be held down," he replies, the sudden stiffness in his shoulders telling me he's realized too late he's just given me a piece of crucial information. Patrick isn't homeless by force or because he has no other choice like me.

"So, you're a runway then?" I ask, shrugging without any judgement. He spears me with a narrowed gaze and continues attending to his fire. Small rivets of smoke flitter towards the sky, and soon enough, the wood is ablaze in a flickering shades of orange.

I should leave it alone, but my curiosity will definitely be my downfall. I drop on my hunches at his side, my knee brushing the heavy coat hanging from his shoulders. "You've probably already guessed where I come from. What's your story?"

"Nothing good comes from living in the past," is the only answer I receive. Patrick stands, leaving me to my own devices while he disappears around the back of the tent for a little while. Not that I'm bothered.

Dragging out one of the many blankets tossed into the tent, I fold it over and place it down beside the fire. Not close enough to be at risk of burning, but enough to feel its warmth. Watching the flames dance and fantasizing what it'd be like to be on the moon, staring down at Earth, fills my time.

"I got you something," Patrick announces, reappearing into view. His body has lost a hundred pounds in clothing; wearing just a simple long-sleeved top and loose fitting lounge pants. His hair is free of the beanie I was sure he'd glued to his head, although the matted brown waves are still flattened down. Running one hand over his small beard, he flashes a packet in the other.

Giant, white marshmallows show around the label, and as Patrick sits a few feet away from me, he pulls two sticks from his pocket.

Skewering a marshmallow for me, Patrick hands it over without looking in my general direction. Sitting upright, I toast the fluffy goodness until it's just brown on all sides and about to drip. Patrick lunges over as I move it towards my mouth, holding out a calloused hand as the marshmallow drops from the stick and seers into his palm.

"Careful," he chastises, but not in a harsh way. "Living rough is dangerous enough. You don't need a burn to contend with." Despite his words, Patrick moves slowly to scrape the sticky fluff onto a piece of the packaging he'd torn off and gives it back to me. Nibbling carefully and blowing when needed, it's not only the marshmallow that's making me feel gooey inside. Patrick acts like he doesn't care, but small glimpses that break through his armor prove otherwise. I wouldn't be in his fortress of tarpaulin otherwise. He could have left me on the side of the road, or let that car hit me, but he didn't.

After a few more marshmallows, I roll out the blanket to lie flat and stargaze. The fire crackles gently at my side, the knot in my stomach finally easing. For the first time since I fled the hospital, I realize I'm actually free. Free of the state's demand on where I live, free of the kids that try to push me around, free of the men who think they own every part of me.

"I could happily stay right here and never leave." I sigh, resting my head on my hands.

"We can't hide up here forever," Patrick replies instantly. Shifting around the rooftop, his shadow looms over me, blocking out the beaming light of the full moon. "The world will forget us if we let them. We need to make some noise just to prove we exist." And that, above all else, is what I take from today.

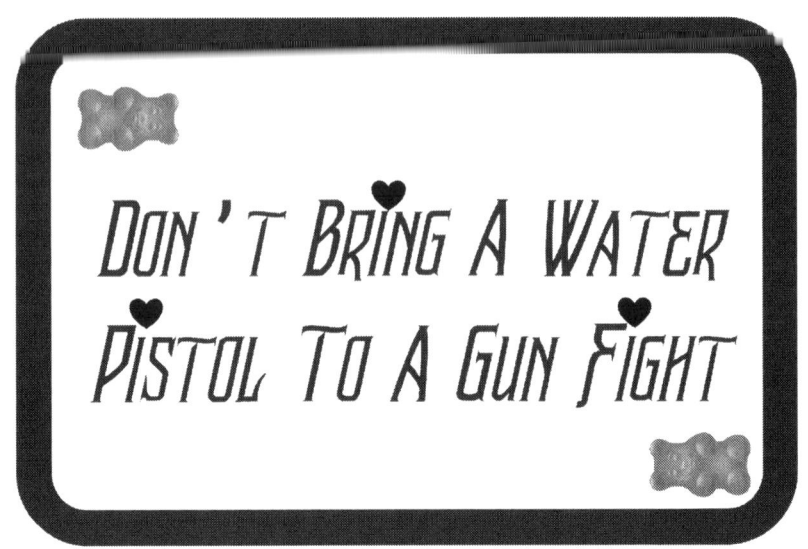

Don't Bring A Water Pistol To A Gun Fight

Fluttering my lids open, I adjust to the morning light, finding myself completely alone. Remnants of our fire trickles across the rooftop in flakes of blackened ash, becoming stuck on the litter strewn all around. Leftover marshmallows spilling from the open packet are beginning to attract attention from an array of birds swooping down onto the roof. Some are bolder than others, not interested in my presence, while the rest hang back on the concrete wall. Starlings swarm the little pillows of joy, their yellow beaks piercing and peaking with intent.

Despite being fascinated by the display, and becoming fully invested in a smaller starling with a bad leg shoving his way to the front, thoughts drift to my own breakfast. I'm certain that not knowing where my next meal is coming from is causing my stomach to demand regular meals, when I know from experience, I can easily go at least two days on the bare minimum. Not wanting to bother my new feathered friends, I crawl out of a gap in the back of the tent and take the fire escape exit. I can't sit around waiting for Patrick to come back and save me every time I need something because there's no doubt in my mind, one day he just won't return.

The street is just as it was last night; still and quiet. The gleam of fresh sunlight reflects off the white walls with blinding accuracy to my retinas. Whether the business folk have headed out early or I've missed the morning school run, there seems to be no one about.

Holding my head high, I walk down the middle of the road, in the direction of the subway station, with one thought present in my mind. Today's agenda—find clothes of my own choosing, and more importantly, shoes.

Just as I witnessed Patrick do multiple times yesterday, I wait for the railway guards to become engrossed in conversation before sneaking beneath the barriers and duck into the first train with open doors to avoid getting caught. The carriage is crammed with suits, answering my question about how early it must be. A man with dreadlocks has a similar idea to me, ride the rails for the sake of some shelter. Except, he has a skill he can make money on, as his fingers strum over the strings of his guitar and he busks right there on the train. Most people ignore him, and even though I clearly have no money to offer his plastic cup, he seems to appreciate my company.

I sit right beside him, tucking my feet beneath my butt and riding the train for as long as he does. Not that I follow him in a creepy way, but the thought of continuing on in silence after he's left doesn't appeal to me. Not with all the judgemental looks we've been getting for nearly the past hour. I do my best to spot which station I started and ended at, although it's hard when the force of the crowd at my back won't let me stand still long enough to read the subway map.

Resurfacing above ground, I spy a serene-looking botanical

garden across the road, framed by a low metal fence. Heading for the entrance gate, I slip inside, intent on losing myself amongst the foliage for a while. For the most part, my morning flies by fairly smoothly. A woman makes it too easy for me, pausing on a park bench while she shouts down the phone at who I imagine is her PA or house slave. When she stands to stomp her tall heel on the concrete, I swoop in and relieve her freshly bought breakfast from the drama. She's already having a bad morning it would seem, and don't bad things always come in threes?

Squatting behind a thick tree trunk, I scoff down the box of blueberry pancakes with extra cream while her shouts, turning around to spread her explicit screams. I want to feel bad, just to prove I'm not losing my conscience, but some people have real problems. Unlike her uncollected dry cleaning that she needs for some fancy party. Like me; I'm starving, shoeless, and a little sweaty with no shower in sight.

At least I have the decency to return her empty container to the bench while she's arguing with a cyclist who happened to ride by too close. Striding away, I sigh in relief and plaster a wide smile on my face. Morning one on my own, and I'd say I'm smashing it.

Wandering through the gardens, I stop by a lake to watch a family of ducks leaving the safety of their nest. A girl and her dad are throwing them chunks of bread, despite the 'Do Not Feed the Ducks' sign right beside them. Letting crucial moments pass, I wonder if my life will always be so ride or die, or if one day I'll get some glimpses of calm. Hell, maybe even the chance at a family of my own creation isn't completely unachievable, but I know for a fact I won't be having kids. There's no way I'll allow a child to enter this cruel world and have the weight of their suffering on my shoulders. I can barely handle my own suffering, thank you very much.

The morning passes and the sun reaches a mid-way point overhead, dipping into the afternoon and signalling I need to get my ass in gear. As beautiful and secluded as certain areas of the park are, the increase in foot traffic is only serving to remind me of today's mission. Leaving the flourishing colors of plants behind, I emerge from the gate I first entered through, careful to not lose my way.

A straight line of shops spreads the other side of the road, too bespoke for my taste, and too expensive not to notice I don't belong there. I walk in the opposite direction, hunting for something more large scale, when I turn the corner and see a huge supermarket. The type that stocks everything from food to DIY, and most importantly, clothes.

Approaching the entrance, I wind around the maze of parked cars, waiting for the precise moment to sweep in. I see it in the form of a crazy woman with a mass of children. Two in a double pushchair and four others trailing behind. Their features and heights are too similar to not be at least one pair of twins, if not more. Ducking into their fold, I slip between a pair of boys just as we cross the threshold into the store. A security guard glances over us and returns to the tiny screen in his security booth. His lack of interest gives me a chance to hang back and spot the four main areas his split screen is focusing on.

"—New lunchboxes, water bottles, and are you boys happy to keep your same backpacks?" The mom with the pushchair turns back, her eyebrows creasing when she spots me. I stop walking, looking around confused myself, as if my family has wandered off. Pointing left, I follow my finger to stride into the completely wrong department and then veer back around to clothing. The girls section is far too vibrant and in-your-face floral for me, although a grey, long sleeved top saying 'My Life, My Rules' does catch my eye.

Walking past, I discreetly yank it from the hanger without stopping and roll it into the baggy hem of my sweater. Heading into the boys section, I do the same to stuff a pair of boys sweatpants into the butt of my full-sized cargos. They shake with each step, bobbing around making my ass look like I'm in a Sean Paul video.

Next, I descend on the shoes, but not the children's shoes. A pair of chunky black boots, much like Patrick's biker ones, are snugly fitted to a six foot mannequin. Silver buckles are fixed to the straps, matching the metal of an inner zip. The best part is, they're unlabelled and de-tagged to fit the plastic feet. Sitting on the podium beside them, I flick the front piece down to sew they are just my size. Never in my life have I been so happy to have big feet.

Propping up one leg and reclining in what I hope is a relaxed position, I begin to lift the non-gender specific piece of plastic, expecting it to be lightweight. It is not. Deceptive like a paperweight, I heave up the calf, causing it to wobble back on its stand while I slide the boot off one foot. The mannequin sways back into place, albeit a little uneven due to the lack of footwear. Then, I twist my body around to tackle the boot on the other side. Just like before, I shift the weight upwards, and just as I'm prying the leather free of its confines, the mannequin falls back with a gigantic crash.

Horrified glances flick my way, the boot sitting in my hand, and I run for it. No one shouts immediately, but the sound of a woman shouting 'that way' has me diving into a clothing rack. Thundering feet race by while my heart beats in my throat, preparing to give out when someone shoves the clothes aside. They don't, and I speedily dress in the clothes and boots. The snug fit takes a moment to adjust to after the loose outfit I've grown used to living and sleeping in. The same one I happily leave in a heap on the floor for someone else to clean up.

Peering out between the sale rack, I spot a stand preparing for the upcoming winter. My gaze snags on a black beanie, a lot like Patrick's, and I smile. Darting out now the coast is clear, I rip out the tag and shove a beanie on my head, hastily braiding my long hair over my shoulder.

Keeping my head down, I spot the same family heading for the exit with their brand new lunchboxes in hand. This time, the twins wear a set of matching dimples and wave me over to slip against their sides as we leave.

"Thanks, guys," I say, saluting and running off before their mom spots me again. She's too busy trying to wrangle her screaming toddlers into their seven-seater anyway. My new boots rub against the lacerations on my feet, but I appreciate the memory foam soles giving me more cushion.

By the time I've returned to the subway station, and ducked past the guard, I'm feeling a thousand times more on top of this homeless life. This time, people on the train don't stare, and a girl further down the carriage even shares a small smile with me.

Retracing my steps, I emerge with my eyes peeled for any sight of Patrick. There's no way to know if he even plans on returning to his rooftop camp tonight, but I hope he does. I want to show him my new look, and more than that, show him how I fared on my own. With a skip in my step, I stroll around for a while longer, trying to decide if it's too early to retreat back. The affluent area doesn't have many stores, considering the amount of flashy cars parked around that can easily drive into the big city.

There is one corner shop that catches my eye though; a

quaint bookstore. Either side of an arched doorway, like a hobbit's home, wood-framed windows highlight the glossy covers inside. Feeling braver in my new outfit that screams I-run-the-world, I push open the door where a small bell chimes. The woman behind the counter is fully invested in a newspaper, barely sparing me a glance.

Veering around a table of best sellers, I follow the polka dots on the floor signaling a one way system around the back of the central counter. Large wooden bookshelves stand tall, leading through the adults section and into the children's. I wouldn't consider myself a child, but an array of magazines, and puzzle and coloring books draw me closer. Who knows how long I'll be up on the rooftop before I find more permanent lodgings.

Collecting a few in my arms that I clearly have no money to pay for, I gasp upon seeing the newest addition in a series I'd started from my old high school library has been released. The Secret of Gladstone Cemetery.

Grabbing a hardback with my greedy hand, a loud slam sounds just before the door chimes again. I drop my stash, ducking low on instinct to peer through the shelves. The angle prevents me from seeing more than a slither of midsections, but I see the glint of a gun clutched in a man's hand. At least four of them barrel inside, with one man shouting at the stunned woman behind the counter.

"Open the till! Now! Do it, or I'll put a bullet between your fucking eyes!" he screams at her. I cover my mouth, a shudder rolling the length of my spine.

Panic I should be equipped to deal with by now sets in, rooting me to the spot as it always does. I try to move my limbs but they hang uselessly, except for the hand clamped on my mouth like a vice. Don't breathe. Don't move and it'll be over soon.

The woman rushes to obey, shoving the contents of her small cashier into the provided bag. There's more cash in there than I thought, but I suppose the area calls for people who want to pay in crisp fifty dollar notes.

Pulling back his bag, the man zips it up harshly and I shift lower to get a look at his face. I shouldn't, because now that face will be embedded in my memory. Tattoos crawl from his neck, up the side of his face and disappear into his hairline. His skin looks like dried wax, caught in the melting process and stuck there. Scars prickle across his cheeks, but nothing like the thick raised line sliced down the right side of his face. In the centre, a hollow white eye gleams straight into my worst nightmares.

"Pleasure doing business with you," he snarls through gold teeth. The other men turn to leave, but not before their apparent boss lifts his gun and shoots the shopkeeper in the forehead. Not even the hand clamped over my mouth can cover up my shocked scream this time, alerting all four men to my presence.

Heads whip my way, their boots moving in an instant, totally ignoring the one-way system. Fight or flight spasms through me like a rocket as I jump to my feet, panicking for something to do. Somewhere to hide. Their shadows loom closer, blocking out the light between the shelves, and I do the only thing I can think of. I shove all of my feeble weight against the unit. Two, three times, I shove with all my might, yet it's useless.

"Oi, you little shit!" one of the men yells, rounding the side of the bookshelf. He has as many tattoos as his boss, but no gun in sight, luckily. Trying to dart away, his fingers brush the length of my braid, clamping on at the last minute to yank me backwards. I screech, holding my head while the man reels me in like a dog on a leash. Pain seizes my scalp, causing another memory to surface through my fear. One I never want to think about again, and one that reminds me I'm done being a victim.

Grabbing the base of my braid, I twist and shout, willing myself free as the others loom closer.

With one last shove of my boot against the books, gravity works in my favor and the shelves begin to sway. My hair is released in favor of trying to stop the cascade of wood, and I tuck it inside my collar. The unit topples and crashes into the next, slamming down one after the other like dominos. The armed men aren't flattened like I hoped, but the books do thunder down on them like fictitious hail and gives me a chance to escape.

Through the gaps in the units, I weave around the crashing books, flying out the door with a brief look back. It's chaos, pure and simple. Luckily the owner isn't alive to see the mess I've created, I think, and then chastise myself.

A guy the same size as the door barrels through it and I scream, running as fast as I can. Pumping my arms, I fly down the street and around the next corner as a car skids to a stop in front of me. Ignoring the driver's shouts, I hunt for the fire escape that will take me to safety. I was sure it was the fifth one on the right, but as I count, the alley doesn't look right. Something's off, my carefully taken mental snapshot not comparing properly.

Without many other options, I race from one to the next, trying to recognize…just anything really. A skid and metal thud rings out behind me, where the same car that almost ran into me before has also nearly handled my gunman problem. Another gunshot echoes and my stomach clenches in a tight knot.

Deciding I need to just get off the road, I take the next alley I see. Using the dumpster handle, I throw myself upwards onto the fire escape, without the need for a ladder. Hopefully if it's still risen, the men won't think to look for me up here.

Taking the steps two at a time, trying not to let my new boots give me away, I spot an open window and without thinking, dive inside. Whatever I find in here must be better than what's waiting for me out there. Squatting low, I peer over the windowsill, just in time to see the men stop and look around. One scratches the back of his neck while the leader thumps another in the head with his gun. Cursing loudly, they continue their hunt and I sag down in relief.

"Erm...hi, again," a voice says behind me and I jerk around, fists raised. They're shaking, but they're ready, just in case. A boy sitting on the end of his bed with a thick textbook in his hand grins at me, one eyebrow cocked over large hazel eyes.

"It's you," I rasp, panting heavily. Just like he did yesterday, the boy flashes a smile of perfectly white teeth and my insides do somersault.

"August," he replies, holding out his hand to greet me formally. Willing myself to stop staring at him, I shuffle forward to take it.

"Candy." Shaking his hand, I risk a glance around at his room. Vinyl records decorate his cream walls, tying into the feature wall. A bold zigzag pattern sits behind a series of mounted guitars. Some are broken, all have been used, and the artwork on most needs a closer look. Aside from the walls, there's not much personality to the room. A simple desk, single bed, wardrobe, huge stack of workbooks, and no technology in sight. His boyband-worthy fringe is too perfectly groomed given the lack of a mirror, until I spot an en-suite bathroom through the next door.

"It's nice to meet you Candy." August brings my attention back with a wink, and the faint blush coloring his cheeks tells me he really means that.

AUGUST OR AWE-GUST?

The girl in the mirror is not one I recognize. My brown eyes are duller, stained with the wash of defeat. Heavy bags that need their own passports hang just beneath my eyes, making the hollowness of my cheeks more obvious. But it's my hair that attracts my lingering stares. Unbraided and hanging over each shoulder, I take a moment in August's en-suite to just think.

I used to take such pride in my glossy, brunette locks, back when I could wash them regularly. Foster homes may be rubbish, but at least there's running water. I'd spend many evenings rhythmically running a brush through the lengths, losing myself in my thoughts. My foster dad's friends would joke I was trying to be Rapunzel, quickly followed by an offer to save me from my 'tower'. The smell of cigar ash finds me as I recall them leering over me, only the burning cherry visible in the dark.

A decision cementing itself in my mind, I begin throwing open drawers beneath the large basin, only stopping when a pair of scissors present themselves to me. Lifting the small pair of handheld shears, I bring them up to a spot just beneath my ear and exhale. No man, whether a trusted friend, or petty thief, will ever use my hair against me like a weapon ever again. And besides, it won't be long before my life on the streets turns the waist-length locks into a matted mess. Fingers twitching, the door opens just as I begin to tighten my grip.

"Candy, do you need— " August stops short in the doorway, his eyes assessing the situation in one easy sweep. Where I think there should be a confused scowl, over the idea I was about to ruin his plush bath mat, a smile appears instead. "Help?" he finishes, moving over to me.

Easing the scissors from my grip, I track him in the mirror as he takes a step behind. My hackles rise, the earlier confidence that had this as the right choice now fleeting me. But, when August reaches over to gently pull the hair tie from my wrist, the brush of his fingers has me remaining ramrod still.

He's a good few inches taller than my five-foot-seven, the faint shadow underlying his jaw suggesting he might be a little older than me. Fifteen, maybe? He's long and gangly, but not in a too-skinny kind of way, and I bet his arms could wrap around me twice in a tight embrace. A flush floods my cheeks as he looks at our reflection, the timing almost as if he could read my mind. Tying my hair into a low ponytail, August waits with a question in his hazel eyes. I nod slightly, holding my breath as he begins to cut just above the hair tie.

What I thought would be panic filling my blood stream, is in fact relief. Each snag I feel tugging at the back of my head is another bad memory being cut away as if it never existed. Once he's freed the mass of hair still bound by the hair tie, August passes it over to me and continues to neaten up the back.

"How do you know how to cut hair?" I ask in a hushed

voice, wiggling the new waves in my hand. August chuckles in his throat, engrossed in his task.

"I don't, really," he says, and my eyes fly up to meet his crinkled gaze. "I do my own fringe because it seems to grow twice as fast as the rest." He shrugs.

Happy with his work, August shifts my hair over each shoulder, just like it was when he walked in. Ignoring the sweep of his knuckles against my neck, although the tingles in my chest definitely *can't* ignore it, I'm pleasantly surprised by my appearance. My hair is longer than I'd expected, reaching just past my shoulders in a surprisingly straight line. I don't know what to say, other than to just stare, and that's when both August and I realize his hands have settled on my shoulder blades.

"You can take a shower, if you like. Or a bath." August clears his throat, taking a step back. "There's a towel on the rack, and use whatever you can find. I don't…get to hang out with many people my age. So…don't feel like you have to run off." He leaves off the 'again' I know is lingering on his tongue and slips back out of the bathroom, like he was never here. This time, I cross the space and flick the lock, resting my back against the wood.

What just happened? My lack of trust just ran away, while I let some boy I've just met brandish a weapon at the back of my neck. Warmth burns in all the areas he touched, and as I draw my fingers through my shortened hair, I can't help but smile. Funny how my world continues to flip on its axis, taking me from abused to homeless, and now in some posh apartment with an N-Sync wannabe. My smile falters when I think of Patrick, and the realization I couldn't find the right fire escape. What if I never find it, and he's sitting up there waiting for me? I should at least head out and look, the tug of my own disloyalty filling my mouth with a bitter taste. But then my eyes settle on the enormous bathtub, and I reckon I could stay just a little while longer.

"Help yourself to whatever you want," August interrupts my snooping, returning from wherever he was when I'd emerged from the longest bath of my life. After going through everything I'd witnessed this afternoon, I just couldn't will myself to get out and face the real world again. The weirdest part is that now the numbness has settled in, I don't feel…anything. It's a trait I'm well practiced in—to block out the bad and convince myself it wasn't real. Apparently, I'm so good at it, not even seeing a woman being shot dead will haunt me. Hell, she might be the lucky one at this rate. I've spent many nights with exploring hands tormenting me in the dark, wishing for death myself.

Shoving the box back beneath his bed, I stand in my stolen clothes and cross my arms. "I wasn't going to…I don't need your charity." I frown, pretending that wasn't a lie. My stubbornness is enough to make it look believable though.

"I didn't mean it like that. Let me rephrase," August states, like a politician in the making. "My dad is a famous rock musician. He spends more time on the road than he does at home, and he thinks sending me hampers of his band's merch makes up for it. Anything I actually wear is in the wardrobe. All of that, I'd rather it went in the trash or…"

"To a homeless girl who crashed through your window?" I finish for him, the fight fleeing my limbs.

"Sounds good to me," he smirks. "Not how I'd expected my day to go. But, for the record, I'm glad you did." It's my turn to smile shyly, diverting my gaze back to my feet. It's not charity if this stuff is going to waste, and let's be honest, rock-style merch—yes, please.

With a shrug, I pull the box back out, and like he said, help myself. Each t-shirt displays a variation of a skull dripping in poison behind its packaging, and when August hands me a backpack, I don't even argue. Being stubborn isn't going to win me any brownie points in life, only deepen my suffering.

"What about your mom?" I ask, dropping down on his bed when I've finished my raid. The textbook he was reading earlier is still sitting open on the covers, presenting reams of biophysics that I'm pretty sure are far beyond high school level.

"She's my dad's business manager—and also on a three month tour with him." August sighs, closing his textbook to take a seat opposite me.

"So…you're here alone?" I ask, flicking my eyes to the closed door and August snorts.

"I wish." He swipes his fringe aside, although the dip to his head causes it to fall right back into his eyes. "If it wasn't for the holidays, I'd still be in boarding school. Instead, I'm under the watch of my nanny, and a rotation of security guards twenty-four seven."

"You have a nanny?" I scoff, before I catch myself. August sweeps his light hazel gaze over my face, an embarrassed chuckle leaving him.

"Don't laugh. Nancy has been looking after me since I learnt to walk. She's live-in, and even comes on holidays to make sure I don't get myself into trouble. We've spent many nights playing board games, and she lets me get away with much more than I should. I can honestly say she knows more about me than my own parents, and she's pretty cool. I think you'd like her."

"Nancy the nanny? I think I'm good." I roll my eyes. I get it's nice August has had someone to care for him when his own parents are too busy, but surely it's also a pain in the ass. The boys around his age that I've lived with are normally out setting fires or trading test answers for cigarettes in the playgrounds.

I glance at the guitars on the wall again, having more context, and twist my lips. On second thought, maybe it's because of this nanny I'm sitting in a comfortable room with a boy who doesn't look at me like a piece of trash. August sure is a rare species, and I told myself just yesterday not to judge so quickly.

"Your loss," August replies with an upturned smile. "Because she just made these, and I thought you might like to try some." Reaching behind him, August produces a plate of small pastry puffs he must have put on his bookshelf on the way in. My stomach jumps up to attention, groaning on cue, and I don't even try to hide it as I accept the plate. Stuffing one into my mouth, I moan loudly. Flavors I can't pinpoint burst in my mouth, a mix of sweet and salty layered evenly between the layers of pastry.

"Okay, maybe I'll give Nancy the nanny a chance." I grin around a mouthful of food. Soon enough, I hand August the empty plate back and recline across the bed. The mattress in the hospital were slabs of rock compared to this, and prior to that… well the privilege of a bed was down to a backyard scrap between me and the new girl, who always came in with the impression she'd be in charge.

The mattress dips and I suddenly realise August is laying by my side. Something that seems innocent enough, but when his hand brushes mine, my heart jackhammers in my chest.

"Candy," August murmurs, and I know he's looking at me. Not trusting my voice, I slide a narrowed look his way that says 'don't try anything stupid'. Not because I don't want him to, but because I don't know where that will leave me in the grand scheme of things. Dumped on the side of the road when he returns to boarding school, no doubt. "Will you tell me what you were running away from when you crashed into my bedroom? You were pale and shaking, so I didn't want to press you. But I'd like to help and keep you safe."

"Why?" I twist my head fully now, becoming absorbed in his beautiful eyes. Specks of darker brown flake his irises, which stand out against his flawless skin. Not a speckle or blemish in sight. I can only imagine he has a vigorous skin care regime, and at this close proximity, I can smell it too. Tea green and water grass, if I were to guess.

Instead of answering my question, August takes my hand in his, on purpose this time, and we just lie there. Staring, holding hands, losing time.

After the longest moment, when sleep threatens to call for me, he shifts. *Closer*. The press of August's arm against mine wakes me back up to super-alert and I suck in a breath. Heat flares everywhere he's touching me, his face nearing. My body yearns to turn into him, my mind reminding me I've just used his toothpaste so I'm all good. Yet, I lie frozen in place. I can't see past his eyes, or the sheltered innocence that lives there. August is pure. I know that with all my soul, and anyone I come into contact with is tainted. Still, as he shifts his face the remaining distance and flutters his eyes closed, all bets are off.

I lay there in wait, a brass band stomping through the center of my chest when a sharp whistle pierces the air outside.

Dodging August's puckering lips, I roll and drop heavily onto the floor beside the bed. Scrambling up, I head to the window and peer out in case those murderous robbers have come back. Cloaked in a heavy jacket, Patrick looks side to side, putting his fingers in his mouth to whistle again. He came back.

"I have to go," I say, excitement and nerves rippling through me as I grab for the backpack. A hand closes around my wrist, but not in an aggressive way.

"You don't have to," August pleads with his large hazel eyes. "I have a sleeping bag we can roll out. It's supposed to rain tonight." His voice trails off, as if he doesn't believe his own lie, spotting the clear sky outside.

"It'll take more than a bit of rain to keep me down." I half-smirk. "I need to get back to my friend before he presumes I'm dead or lost." Maybe classing Patrick as a friend is jumping ahead, but he saved my life and showed me ways to carry on. Both are invaluable, and I'm nothing if not loyal. There's no way I can ditch him now for a night sleeping on someone's floor. Someone I don't really know, if I'm being honest.

Easing my wrist from August's grip, I shove the bag on my back and throw a leg out of the window.

"Will I see you again?" The question comes, tugging at my torn heart. I understand loneliness, better than anyone, but I also know nothing good can come from August having me close by. One day, my demons will catch up with me and I need to be ready for when that happens, not curled up in a sleeping bag and stolen clothes.

"For your own good, I really hope not," I breathe, exiting his room and jogging down the fire escape. Calling out, Patrick retraces his steps after he'd disappeared from view. I reach the end of the escape as he comes to stand beneath it and holds out his arms. Jumping from the edge, I land in Patrick's arms before thinking about the possibility of him not catching me.

"Where have you been, little one?" he asks, setting me down.

His eyes roam over my backpack and as I look up at the window, August's shadow looms behind the glittering curtain.

"Acquiring new clothes," I shrug honestly. Shaking my boot at him, Patrick lets out a sound of appreciation and leads me onto the fire escape directly opposite. Dammit, I knew I was close, but I'd mixed up my lefts and rights.

"I would warn you against stealing this close to the base, but I'm too damn impressed. Here I was thinking you'd just sit on the roof all day waiting for this." Flashing me a plastic bag that's steaming and releasing a heavenly smell, I smile cockily.

"I'm not the type to wait around for a savior." I grin as Patrick gives me a boost up to grab the ladder.

"I can see that." His lingering gaze sends a prickle up my back, a mini alarm sounding in the back of my head. I shove down the discomfort, reminding myself Patrick has been nothing but good to me—even if it has been by forcing me to learn the hard way.

Making it up to the rooftop camp, I drop onto a crumpled blanket with a relieved sigh. I made it back in one piece. Patrick lays out tubs of Chinese food I know he didn't buy and holds out a plastic spoon. When I try to take it, he maintains his grip so we're both reaching over the food.

"Here's to you, little one. To a day well lived." He nods and releases the spoon. The smile that spreads across my face could crack my jaw from my cheeks. I like that—a day well-lived. If only Patrick knew the truth about where I've been and what I've seen today, but he was new to the streets once. We do what we have to. Patrick dives into a chow mein, nudging a box of chicken fried rice my way. I don't have the heart to tell him I already ate, and I'm by no means too full to appreciate a decent meal when I've got one sitting in front of me.

After dinner, we call it an early night. The sky is still a mix of deep blues and purples, spanning across our undisturbed horizon. Wriggling into a ball on the covers, my body aches for the comfort of August's mattress, and that in itself is the problem. Too quickly could I become accustomed to being cared for, and as soon as I allow that—I'm a goner. I need the tough lessons, the valuable teachings that Patrick provides. In the name of survival, it's the only way.

I'm Your Boyfriend Now, Nancy

Once again, I awake to Patrick missing and that sick feeling in the pit of my stomach. Is this how it'll always be? A good night followed by a day of being alone, getting up to who knows what, and running the risk of not making it back each time. Instead of running that risk, and contrary to what I said yesterday, I spend most of the day hanging out on the rooftop.

Police have cordoned off the bookshop down the street, but a lapse in patrolling when I ventured out for breakfast meant I could sneak in and grab those books I'd dropped. Snatching a few packs of pens and colors scattered across the floor means I've remained stretched out beneath the uninterrupted sunshine, doodling and testing my trivia skills. The rest of the puzzle books, and that hardback I craved, are stashed into the backpack, where all my supplies now live.

Chewing on a cereal bar August must have forgotten was in his backpack, dinner time rolls closer with no sign of Patrick. I'm going to have to leave the safety of this rooftop again, but my tired legs really don't want to. Not that they've done much exercise today, but I'm just tired and bored of a life I have to obtain for myself. Where's the luck that finds others so easily? And besides, after I told August I hope he doesn't see me again, I feel like I've set myself a standard to live up to. It's for his own good. Yet, I can't lay around and starve, then no one will be seeing me again.

Pushing myself upright, I take a little more time than necessary on my appearance. There's an external tap hidden behind the tarp tent which I use to wash before dressing and combing my fingers through my shortened hair. It drips onto the black t-shirt, this one with an ice cream cone upside down on the skull's head. Pulling on the sweatpants I roughly washed, beat against the wall, and left out to dry, I venture down the fire escapes, backpack firmly in place. Jumping the rest of the way to the ground, I've barely made it out of the alley when I hear my name being called.

"Hey, Candy!" I close my eyes briefly, stealing myself for the one interaction I wanted to avoid. Spinning slowly, I see August on the opposite sidewalk, waving from behind his black BMW GT. "We're going to the Drive-In Cinema. Wanna come?" I pause, my eyes flicking from the bulky man, getting ready to slide in behind the wheel, to the woman closing the truck, frowning at me slightly. She's middle-aged, still rocking flared jeans that show off her long legs, with a floral blouse on top. Her whitish-blonde hair is wispy, escaping a casual bun on the back of her head.

I look from one end of the street to the other, not noticing anyone else as I tentatively slink across the road.

"Nancy, this is Candy," August introduces us, moving around to join my side. "We play doubles at badminton sometimes. She has a mean smash shot," he chuckles at his own lie. I smile too, pretending to share the inside joke.

"Ummm. It's okay with me, if your parents don't mind." Her blue eyes glance back at the fire escape, it looks like I've just used to sneak out, and I shake my head. "Well, alright. As long as you can convince Carl she's not some assassin." Nancy rolls her eyes with a smile. The atmosphere dissipates when August opens the door for me to slide into the back seat and follows just behind. Nancy takes the passenger seat, giving Carl a soft smack when he grumbles about my presence and I warm to her immediately.

Ignoring the hard stare the bald security guard gives me in the rear-view mirror, I watch the world pass behind the safety of the blacked-out windows. Secretively, I'm keeping an eye out for Patrick, but the odds of him being nearby are slim to none. He has the whole city at his beck and call. The further we venture, the more I fill with excitement. I'm in a new-plate car, going to my very first cinema drive-in with a cute boy at my side. This is totally how normal thirteen-year olds spend their summer break. More worried about their nails than where their next meal will come from.

The radio is cranked up at August's request—some heavy head-banging rock, and I wonder if it's his dad's band. He nods along like this is easy listening, while my body shakes to the beat involuntarily. Sharing a small smile, we return to our sightseeing out the windows until the BMW is pulling into the Drive-In entrance. A red flashing arrow directs us inside, the light box beneath showing tonight's pick; 'Nightmare on Elm Street'.

It's already quite busy, but the parking warden directs us through the maze to the front. Special bays reserved for the fancy cars are backed by bunting, where the common folk park in any which way they like. Some pick-ups reverse in so people can bundle in with blankets and my lips twist. I should probably be back there, but as August stretches a hand out, it doesn't occur to me not to take it. Nancy is setting out a row of camping chairs, signaling for me to take the one on the end. It only makes sense August would be between us, while Carl hangs back in the driver's seat with the door popped and one leg hanging out.

"There's a food truck over there. What can I get you guys?" Nancy asks, pushing her hands into her back jeans pockets.

"Oh, I didn't bring any money." I duck my head, but Nancy merely laughs softly.

"It's not often August gets to go out with friends outside of school. Please, whatever you want—it's on us." By us, I presume she means August's parents, and that's something I can get on board with. Leaving their son behind while they tour the world for months at a time, they won't miss a few extra dollars out of their deep pockets.

"We'll take whatever they've got. I'm starving." August agrees with my growling stomach and Nancy leaves with a wink. I slink down into the chair, wondering how much of our conversation Carl is listening into. All of it probably.

"Doesn't it feel weird, having someone running all of your errands?" I ask, twiddling my thumbs.

"Ha," August replies dryly. "I've tried many times to pull on the leash around my neck, but Nancy takes it as a personal insult. If she's not proving she's doing her job, she gets all fidgety, and next thing I know, my boxers are all ironed and folded into little swans." I burst out laughing, covering my mouth too late to block out a snort. The massive screen before us bursts to life, displaying a range of advertisements while all I can picture is August's origami underwear.

Drowning out my laughter, a trailer begins to play and it's

not lost on me how August shuffles his chair closer before settling back. I try to focus on the screen, but my betraying eyes keep trailing back to the fingers knotted over his stomach. The same ones that held my hand so gently, promising me things that can never be. This isn't some live-action version of Lady and the Tramp. Guess which one I am.

Nancy returns just before the movie starts, handing us a large pizza box to share, and removes the popcorn tub handles from her arm. Beneath her clenched bicep, she takes the cans of coke that she'd squished there against her ribs. Happy we're all sorted, Nancy finally pulls the box of jellybeans out of her back pocket and sits with a contented sigh, popping one into her mouth.

"I hope you're not scared of horror movies," August leans over to mutter. The mirth on his face tells me he already knows the answer to that question, and I lift the piece of pizza he was going for from the box.

"Why? Are you offering to hold my hand if I am?" I ask sarcastically, not knowing where that came from. The glint in August's eyes tells me he wouldn't mind, but I'm all too aware of the security guard staring at the back of my head.

Stuffing my mouth with pizza and turning back to the movie, I don't pay any attention to the flare of heat flooding my cheeks. From the first jump scare and August's stifled snigger, I'm fully engrossed in the screen. I'm not an avid movie watcher, since that requires the use of a television. Something I didn't have access to, or access to any technology for that matter, aside from some bulky computers in my old school library, and even they came with restricted access. My heart is racing, the anticipation of when the knife-fingered villain will strike again smothering out any thoughts of boys and soppy notions.

"Well…" I breathe, slumping back in my chair as the end

credits roll. I hadn't realized I had grown so stiff, a half-eaten tub of popcorn in my lap that August must have unwrapped and swapped out while I wasn't paying attention. Didn't stop me from eating them though, the saltiness lingering around my teeth. Puffing my cheeks out, I turn to find him staring at me, fully engrossed in my reaction.

"Too scary?" he mocks with a cocked eyebrow.

"You wish." I laugh. "You'll have to hold your own hand instead." My eyes stray from August to a spot beyond his head. A group of men have congregated a little further down the strip, all of their bodies angled towards me. I tell myself it's a trick of the light, but when one last flash and a high-pitched scream bursts from the movie screen, it's undeniable they're staring straight at me.

I jolt, along with the rest of the audience, August included, but I don't lose sight of the men. Their eyes linger, their hands dipping into dark jean pockets. The hair on the back of my neck stands on end and a small voice in the back of my head tells me to move out this damn camping chair and run. But it's when the group of men step out of my eyeline behind the cars, that I really start to panic. A threat I can see is much more preferred than one which is stalking around, their shadows nearing the BMW behind me.

"I need to use the bathroom," I announce, shooting upright. August chuckles and Nancy tries to hide her giggle, as I realize they believe the after-credits jump scare just made me pee my pants. Taking that excuse over reality, I dart away towards a semi-circle of temporary toilets. There's a long line of people waiting, but I run to the front, slipping into a door that's just being opened.

"Sorry! Desperate!" I shout as they all begin to moan. Slamming the door closed as soon as the woman leaving gets out of the way, I slam the lock shut and steel myself. It's just the movie. The stupid scary movie has made me think there's even more monsters roaming around.

Inhaling deeply, the horrid stench of an unflushed toilet pollutes my lungs and I cough heavily. Lifting the t-shirt hem to cover my mouth, headlights pass outside, highlighting my worst nightmare. Every side of the plastic box I'm inside is surrounded by a large silhouette and if it wasn't for the hand over my mouth, I would have screamed.

"Are you sure it's her?" a deep voice rumbles through the plastic walls and into my very soul. With the light gone, I'm plunged back into almost darkness inside the blue box that's become my prison. A grunt comes from beside him, making me spin towards the back.

"The resemblance is uncanny."

"We've been wrong before," the left side says. "I'm not in the business of burying children for no reason." Dread claws up the inside my throat, acidic-like bile that just sits there.

"When you don't get paid, you mean," the first man grumbles. Breathing in tiny pants through my nostrils, I begin to shake. The man at the doorway has yet to speak, and without knowing if he's still there or not, I'm trapped. I can't imagine men lurking at a drive-in are state officials, and they didn't resemble any of the guys I saw shoot up the bookstore. So I can only imagine these men are hunting for me on my foster father's orders.

Tears escape my eyes, forcing me to release the t-shirt and push the heels of my palms into my eyes. I hate showing weakness, even in the dark on my own. But if they're here to drag me back, that's it for me. I won't survive another day in his care, not now I've royally pissed him off.

"Can I help you gentlemen?" a voice sounds, and I raise my

head. No answer comes, but a moment later, a loud thump sounds against the edge of the plastic. I gasp, throwing myself against the basin, as if that will help. Another thud comes and it's obvious a fight is breaking out beyond the door. The mix of grunts and yells confuse me until I don't know where the sounds are coming from. All I know is, I need to get out of here.

Taking my shot, I unlock the door and bolt for it. Bodies are nearby, but not close enough, as I push my legs as fast as possible. The toilet queue has dispersed into a crowd, gasping at the fight taking place behind me. Another second and a slam draws my attention back to the temporary toilet, which is now laying on its side. Heaving out a breath, I keep going until the pounding of footsteps speeds up behind me. A hand grabs the back of my t-shirt and I scream, digging my nails into the hand.

"Candy! It's me, Carl!" the security guard hisses, as I scratch the skin clean off the top of his hand. Allowing him to sweep me up under his arm, Carl carries me at top speed back towards the BMW. I'm grateful that he passes around the back of the next car along and stuffs me inside, before announcing to August and Nancy that it's time to go. Code Griffin, he calls it.

On instinct, August rushes into the seat beside me and Nancy jumps into the front, leaving the camping chairs as we peel out of the parking bay. Blaring his horn, Carl doesn't stop for anyone as people jump out of his way, and I swear, no one breathes until we're back on the road with nobody following us.

Stretching out a hand, I link my fingers with August's, no questions asked. I'm still shaking, but the way he rubs the back of my hand and gives me a reassuring smirk, I can tell he thinks the threat was against him. Little does he know, Carl just saved me from a serious situation. Something's definitely going on here, and I'm not sure I want to know what it is.

HOT WIRE VS LIVE WIRE

It's fair to say, at this point, my morals have well and truly gone out of the nearest window. After Carl insisted I stay over following the drive-in, it became harder and harder to say no when August kept rolling out the sleeping bag. I was just thankful Carl didn't tell the others about the men who were clearly after me. I've thought about it night after night, alongside wondering if Patrick has given up waiting for me yet. I'm sure he'll understand, as soon as I get back to explain I've been receiving three meals a day, regular showers, and decent companionship. Anyone in my position would have done the same.

Returning to the apartment, Carl holds open the front door and waits for us to pass through. He lives in the apartment across the hall, close enough to keep an eye on visitors and the building's surveillance, without him hovering over August's every move. I say my thanks, bobbing in the badminton outfit Nancy insisted I would need to join August's weekly session. It's not lost on me how she hasn't asked once why I'd be sleeping on August's floor, since I supposedly lived across the road, nor does she presume I won't be here for dinner.

"You can use my shower again, Candy," she tells me from the kitchen. "You kids go freshen up. I've made my speciality—ham and leek pie." I smile back before she disappears behind the cupboard she's rummaging through. Passing through her bedroom, I find another fresh set of clothes waiting for me on the counter by the basin. Neatly folded with the tags hanging out. I sigh with a smile, wondering just how it is I lucked out. I know it can't last forever, considering summer break is coming to an end soon, but I push that thought to the back of my mind.

Showering with Nancy's expensive shower cremes and shampoo, I work up a lather in the steam before letting it all melt away. It's becoming easier to leave the comfort of the hot water, now it's not such a rarity, wrapping myself in a thick towel to assess the clothes. A sporty outfit in navy and gold makes me grin—practical and fashionable at the same time. The best part about being shopped for is that Nancy doesn't need to be told my size or preferences. She just *gets it*.

After dressing and brushing my hair out, I leave the safety of the bathroom when voices filter my way. I pause just behind Nancy's bedroom wall, listening in as one voice makes the hair on the back of my hair stand up. Oh sh—

"Candy, sweetheart? Is that you?" Nancy calls, and I scrunch my eyes closed. Blowing out a breath, I slink out of my hidden spot and head for the kitchen. "You have a…um, visitor." I don't need Nancy's introduction, as Patrick's eyes blaze a trail from my fitted leggings and sweater, to my freshly washed hair. Despite the tightness to his jawline, his voice comes out almost sincere.

"I've been looking everywhere for you, little one. Was starting to think the worst, until I saw you heading into this apartment block." Removing his beanie, Patrick runs a hand through his matted hair. Mud coats his usually shiny boots, his tatty coats hanging past the ripped holes in his jeans. There's no sense of fashion present, just overworn and threadbare clothing that are in dire need of replacing.

"Yeah, I'm sorry—I didn't mean to—"

"Don't mention it," Patrick cuts me off. The twitch to his nostrils betrays the nice act he's trying to put on. "I just wanted to make sure you were okay. But it looks like you are, so I guess I'd better leave you be?" His question hangs in the air, holding so much more weight than Nancy probably perceives. She takes her cue, returning to her pie while tossing curious glances our way. Sighing, I hang my head and resign myself to the inevitable.

"No, it's fine. I'm ready to leave now," I say, catching Patrick's raised eyebrow from beneath my lashes. A clutter sounds as Nancy drops her utensil and whips around to my side.

"You don't have to do anything you're not comfortable with, sweetheart," she tries to whisper, but Patrick snorts. Turning his back, he strides out of the doorway Carl is lingering in, keeping his foot jammed against the door. "We can work something out." Nancy tries again, gently tugging on my arm. I twist my face to hers, willing myself not to cry.

"Tell August goodbye for me," I say, and tear myself away from her concerned frown. Before letting me go, Nancy pushes the backpack strap into my hand, being her usually thoughtful self. Leaving my heart behind in the apartment, Carl nudges my fist on the way passed and tells me to take care of myself. It's hard to do when my heart is being so easily swayed with the promise of a home, while my head is screaming to protect myself long term. I can't depend on others to care for me if I can't do it for myself. I need to find my own way, not leech off August. He's too good to have me dragging him down, and will probably forget about me as soon as he returns to boarding school anyway.

Tracing Patrick's footsteps down the staircase, he doesn't acknowledge me until we are outside and out of view. When he turns, it's with the lingering venom I know he was struggling to hold back in front of others.

"Did you have a nice vacation?" he sneers, and I swallow down a lump of guilt.

"I'm sorry," I repeat, not sure what else to say. Every self-centred argument deserts me under the scrutiny of his hard stare.

"Mmmm, well that's just fine then," Patrick tuts sarcastically. "And to think, I was looking for you because I discovered some information you'd probably like to know. Unless you already do, and the whole orphan thing was bullshit too." I wince at his curse, keeping my head low like a dog being disciplined.

"You asked if I was from an orphanage, not if I was an orphan. If I have parents, I have no idea who or where they are," I mutter. It all seems moot now, a physical part of me feels like it's missing. I could slap myself for being so stupid. What did I think would happen—I'd sneak in August's suitcase and live in his dorm room? I never should have stayed and I definitely shouldn't have gotten attached.

"Hey," Patrick says, softer this time. I flinch when his fingers touch my chin, having played this game many times before. *Look at me when I'm talking to you*, *take your punishment like a good girl*. Yet the lack of anger in Patrick's face slips through my defences, and the first tear I was holding back falls. "Wherever you've gone, it's time to come back to the present. I have news on your mom. More than that, I have an address if you're interested?

The air locks in my lungs as I stare up, blinking a few times. Meet my mom? That was a young girl's dream that I'd given up on long ago. The shame I'd felt when Patrick called for me at the apartment washes away as hope blooms in its place. Maybe it's not too late for me yet? Maybe I can have a place to belong after all.

"Where is she?"

"Na-ah." Patrick's mouth lifts in one corner. "Information like that isn't easy to come by. You need to do a favour for me first, to prove you're still loyal to the streets. Can't have you using me and running off again. It's not good for my reputation to be taken for a ride." I nod in understanding, becoming more and more desperate for the carrot he's hanging just out of my reach. Also, I've had enough fake foster brothers to understand the male ego isn't something easily patched up. I've hurt Patrick, and in return, he's going to make me jump through a few hoops.

"What do you want me to do?"

My gut churns with nerves. I'd been so confident earlier, when I thought Patrick's request was going to be easier. Or at least far enough away from posh street that my heart wouldn't be beating in my throat. Squatting behind the dumpster in our opposite alley, we waited out the sun setting whilst chewing on the gum I stole and Patrick never used. Now darkness has settled, and I feel like every mouthful is about to come back up.

"It's time," Patrick states. "Just like I told you." Placing a long piece of thin metal in my hand, he nudges me out of our hiding spot. I stumble forward on numb feet, my prized boots failing me as I drop them forward step by step. They don't feel half as special or comfortable anymore; not now I see them for what they really are. A reminder of the life I'm supposed to lead. A thief. A worthless, reckless thief that should have made better choices. Not that I have any choice in what I'm about to do. As I glance over my shoulder, I see Patrick's shadow urge me forward.

Sneaking across the road, I duck behind the BMW GT that I so recently became accustomed with. Ragged breaths saw in and out of me, my limbs too heavy to move. Of all the cars on the block, why did it have to be this one? Although, I know why. Patrick wants to prove a point. Never trust a street rat who has nothing to lose.

Not wanting to wait for witnesses to appear, I push up on my knees and slide the metal rod in between the window and door jam. Shimmying it the way Patrick told me to. I have no faith in this plan, until the headlights blink and the door unlocks with a suspicious double beep. Hmmm, that's not how Patrick described it, but I'll take the win. Sliding inside the driver's seat, I wriggle down into the footrest and look for the outline I need to open. Pop.

Next comes the pen knife Patrick gave me to keep in my boot. Snagging through the wires, I wince and hide my face as I spark them together. The engine roars to life beneath me, and a relieved exhale flies from the depths of my lungs. Thank the lord for that. I might make it out of this unscathed after all, and Patrick can think again if he believes I'll stick around after he's given me the address to my mom. I'm done with this life. There has to be something better waiting for me.

Dropping back into the seat, I have to drag it right up to the wheel, and even then I need to lean forward enough to see through the windscreen. It occurs to me too late, I don't know how to drive a car, and as I look around for Patrick to help me, he's nowhere to be seen—as usual.

It can't be too hard. I've snuck onto GTA on my foster brother's PlayStation in the middle of the night dozens of times. Pressing my foot down on the accelerator, the car leaps forward, and I quickly press my foot on the brake. Assessing myself for damage, when my chest feels like it's fit to explode, I shake my head in despair. Get a grip, Candy.

This time, I press my foot down, gripping the wheel when the car flies forward. I hold my breath the entire time, a mere 'ah haha!' tearing from me as the end of the street nears. I'm doing it. I'm going to get away with this. Just then, a pair of headlights blind me, and I scream at the top of my lungs. Slamming my foot down on the brake hard, I scrunch my eyes closed and twist the steering wheel to skid sideways, the scream never ending. With a rough jolt against the wheel, that will definitely bruise, I finally stop and drop my head back against the headrest.

"Carl?" a woman's voice asks, and my eyes fly open. A woman is peering into the window with her hands clamped around her eyes. Realizing I'm not Carl, she curses and rips the door open. "What the…Who the hell are you?"

"Mrs Harrington!" the real Carl shouts, running up the street. "It's not what it looks like. Candy here is a friend of August's, and I was…just…I let her…"

"Steal my car?" Mrs Harrington finishes for him with a cocked eyebrow. I mirror the expression, stepping out of the seat with my hand held up for him to stop.

"Please, don't take the blame for me," I say, tears welling in my eyes. "It's okay. I'll probably be better off in prison anyways."

"I should think so." Mrs Harrington lifts her head towards the sky. "It might teach a little scoundrel like you a lesson in respecting people's property." Pulling her phone out of her back pocket, the screen brightens her face. A pinched nose bridges between her stark, blue eyes and painted lashes. The fingers clasping her phone stretch out their manicured talons, close enough to stab me in the eye if I'm not careful. I swallow thickly, feeling the heat of eyes weighing down on me as people emerge from their homes to see what all the commotion is about. I don't pay them any mind. At least it's not—

"Mom! Wait!" August calls, and for the first time, I hang my head in shame. Of all the people, he's the one I didn't want to see me like this. Caught red-handed, hotwiring his family car, after they've been nothing but generous and welcoming to me. "Don't call the cops. No one is hurt, and there's no damage caused. Please, give her another chance." Coming to stand beside me, the brush of August's arm causes me to shift aside and avoid his gaze.

"August, go back inside. I will handle this," his mother tells him sharply, but he doesn't move. A man emerges from the vehicle facing the side of the BMW, effectively blocking me in, if I were stupid enough to attempt an escape.

"Everyone okay?" the man asks, and I know instantly, he must be August's dad. The image of a rocker, his hair is long like August's, more than likely in the same shade of darkened brown. Tattoos cover every inch of his visible skin, up to his jawline, and the baggy t-shirt hangs from his stick-thin frame.

"No, we are not okay. Our son is taking the side of some

criminal that just tried to steal our car, over his own mother, who he hasn't seen in months."

"And who's fault is that?" August seethes back, in a tone that surprises me. I flick my wide eyes to his mother, gauging her shocked reaction before she locks it down. Sidestepping, August bravely takes my hand, refusing to let go when I try to retract from it. "You haven't been here, so there's a lot you don't know. Let Candy leave and we'll talk about this inside."

Two things strike me in that moment—Firstly, the caring nature of a boy who would fight his own parents to see me walk away unscathed, and secondly, the sway a neglected child has with his parents. Narrowing her eyes into slits, Mrs Harrington glares from our clasped hands to my face.

"Get out of here, and don't let me see you again." With a sharp nod and the release of August's hand, I turn and run, pushing past Carl and ignoring the crowd that's gathered all around. Tears skewering my vision, I don't stop at the alley way that I know all too well. I don't stop at the next intersection, as horns blare and driver's scream at me to watch where I'm going. Only when the light of the subway station obscures the thoughts of self-hatred echoing around my mind, do I finally pull my pounding boots to a stop. And who else should I find there, leaning against the railing, none other than Patrick.

"How'd you get on, kiddo?" he asks, and I growl at him. That pet name is a hard-no for me.

Wiping my tear-stained cheeks, hard enough to scratch them on the button from my sleeve. I glower, as if I could melt Patrick through sheer will.

"I got into the damn car—" I start, only to be interrupted by his harsh laugh.

"I know that bit. Who do you think unlocked the door for you?" Pulling his hand from his large overcoat, Patrick shakes a

BMW key fob at me, and my mouth drops open. He must have lifted it from Carl when leaving the apartment, and set up this whole plan for my humiliation. Or was it to make sure I'd never see August again?

"You had that the whole time?! What was the point of making me—"

"To prove a point." He interrupts me for the second time, clearly not wanting a two-way conversation—just an ego-boost. "I don't put my trust in others often, and when it's broken—you need to earn it back. I'd say we're back on the same playing field now, wouldn't you?" I don't answer in favor of striding past with my head held high. Screw this.

A hand covered in fingerless gloves latches onto my chin, tugging my face around to face his dangerous glare. "Don't think you can walk away from me, little one. I've invested too much in you."

The demand for an explanation burns on the tip of my tongue, but I hold it in. That's what Patrick wants—for me to take the bait and beg him for answers. It may have taken me too long to realize that, but now I can make sure I never give him the satisfaction.

Shoving my face aside, it's Patrick's turn to push past, his coat tails flapping around his calves as he disappears further down the subway steps.

"You coming?" he shouts back, his voice bouncing around the concrete walls. "You've just had a fun meeting with your boyfriend's mom. Don't you think it's time you're reunited with your own?"

Spank My Ass and Call Me Thirsty

Of all the cliché endings I dreamt up for myself, standing before a strip club in the roughest part of town wasn't one of them. The two days it took Patrick to hear from his informant friend, gave me plenty of chances to catch up on my sleep, in various bus shelters and subway stations. I haven't spoken to Patrick much beyond telling him when I'm going to find a bathroom, or accepting the food he's stolen for us with a muttered thanks. At least he had the good sense to bring my backpack along. Although, he helped himself to my rock band t-shirts and my stashed snacks, as if they were his own.

"Well," Patrick says. "Are we going in, or are we just going to stand here?" I glance over the strip club's exterior again. A swirling neon sign labels this place as the 'Thirsty Kirsty', and besides that the light flashes over the outline of a woman upside down on a pole, her legs blinking from open to closed and back again. As subtle as a tornado. Not able to gauge anything else from the outside, I huff and walk inside without another thought. All expectations of a warm welcome have vanished, but I've come this far, I might as well see it through.

Despite it being a bright morning outside, the interior of the club is dark and dingy. It occurs to me, the lack of windows permits this, with strips of red tube lights framing the long room. The stage spanning the opposite end splits into three sections, each with a personal walkway and pole fixed at the end. For the handful of sleazes in here, there's one single woman slowly easing herself around the pole in time with the music. A shimmering red bikini just about holds in her boobs, and slips up the rear of her ass, matching the feather boa strewn over her shoulders. Shifting my gaze away from her fantastic set of abs, long brown hair flows from her scalp, and beneath the mask of make-up, it's hard to get an accurate gauge on her age.

"Is that…" I breathe, biting down on my bottom lip. Patrick's hands settle on my shoulders, and he twists me, his mouth coming too close to my ear.

"Guess again," he whispers, stopping me in front of a lengthy bar. The glass shelves behind are bare, and the stools in front of the glittery black surface are empty, as my eyes scan for a hint of life. Suddenly, she pops up from where I imagine the glasses in her hands are stored. The first thing that strikes me is her height—shorter than me, even at my age. Her chestnut brown hair hangs to her middle like a curtain. Then there's the curves for days—a perfect hourglass figure in a tiny dress, and a set of wide hips I surely won't inherit. I'm too tall and gangly, to the point I question if we are related, but then she turns and I can't deny the resemblance in our faces. Rounded with a small upturn to her nose, and large chocolate eyes that match mine. Wow. She's actually gorgeous and full, in all the right ways.

Not sensing our presence, she twists to pop the glasses in their rack and goes about her business wiping down the bar while Patrick pushes at my back. He's good at nudging me where he wants to go, but when I step back to lean on him, he disappears.

Stumbling aside, I slam my hand down on the bar to balance myself, and those brown doe eyes swing my way. There's some hesitation in her brows at first, but an easy smile soon sweeps across her face and she walks over to me.

"You lost, sugar?" She leans on the counter, tossing the damp cloth aside. "Or maybe just hungry? I can fetch you some chips, if you like." She winks and words fail me. She's pretty…and nice. That doesn't sound right, because why the hell would she not have looked for me before now? Surely, a life beside her, even one involving a strip club, would have been better than what I've had to endure. Following her eye line, I turn my left arm over, to show the crook of my elbow and the heart-shaped birthmark stamped there. I decided a long time ago, that the second I turn eighteen, that's the first place I'm having tattooed. It's too ironic a girl with no love in her life would be mocked by her own blemishes. That's when her face falls, the realization of who I am setting in.

"Surprise." I shrug, not knowing what else to do with myself. All friendliness vanishes as her face visibly pales and she begins to shake her head.

"You can't be here," she hisses, taking a few steps back. I follow her, not ready to let go so soon after meeting her.

"Why? Don't you…want me?" I croak out, my fears coming to life. I knew this was a terrible idea, yet I let Patrick convince me it was the right time. She shakes her head again, and dammit, my false hope plummets like a brick in the pit of my stomach.

Calling for a nearby waitress, the woman who birthed me whispers harshly for me to be fed and then shown the door, before she disappears out back. I watch the door slam closed, my arms limp at my side. A wolf whistle draws my attention to the front of the stage, where the stripper's chest is now fully exposed, crawling on her hands and knees towards a cheering Patrick. Jutting her ass in and out, she slowly turns like a cat while Patrick robs the dollars from her thong.

A menu is pushed in front of me by the waitress, a blonde not much older than me. The laminated leaflet contains a handful of side orders that I imagine are microwaved. Not that I'm a prude, but I couldn't eat now if I tried. Instead, I turn and head for the door, my steps heavier than ever. What am I doing? Chasing pipe dreams, reopening closed wounds, and welcoming punishments I did nothing to earn. It's time for a new path. A direction of my own making, but I have a few ties to shake loose first. And a goodbye to say, to the only person who has ever genuinely cared for me. My sweet August.

That UNO Reverse Shit

Lifting my hand, my knuckles hover over the wooden door when it bursts open.

"You came back!" August almost cries, whipping me up into a tight hug. I freeze in his hold before melting completely, laying my head on his shoulder. He smells of tea-tree and mint, the combo that invades my senses and fills me with butterflies. Placing me back on my feet, I smile warmly, when a heavy hand lands on my shoulder and I flinch.

"Good to see you again." Carl inclines his bald head. The open door at his back explains his sudden appearance, probably having watched me drag my feet all the way up the stairs. "We can cancel the private investigator. You're a tricky girl to hunt down." Blinking twice at his retreating back, I gape at August.

"He's joking, right?" Rubbing a hand over his nape, the boyband wannabe shrugs shyly.

"Well...I couldn't find you up on the rooftop I've seen you climb down from, and I...um, worried." I can't be mad at the blush coating his flawless face. Once again, his boyish good looks and sweet nature slips beneath my defenses, reminding me there's still good people in this world. "My mom was the one who suggested the PI, after I explained everything to her. She's really sorry about what she said. Jet lag and nightly rock festivals aren't a good mix." August ducks his head apologetically. I don't have time to process this information before his smile reappears and he tugs me inside the apartment.

"No, wait! I wasn't going to stay," I try, but he's not listening. Nancy is bustling behind the kitchen counter when she spots me and drops everything to run over. Throwing her arms around me too, I could almost choke up at the reception I didn't expect.

"Oh, Candy darling! It's great to have you back. I'll set an extra place for dinner." She's gone before I can protest, and at this point, I really don't want to. No one has worried for my safety like this before, but as August pulls me into the main living area, the fuzzy feeling vanishes.

I've been in here before, but in all the other times, the room hasn't been filled with the icy temperature I notice now. Splashes of gold stand out against regal green wallpaper, from the vases holding huge house plants to the glimmering chandelier. Sitting bolt upright on the chaise lounge, Mrs Harrington looks every bit the business manager, while August's dad is stretched out, his head on her lap. They're like the yin and yang of each other, but it must work for them.

"Hey mom, look who's back," August says proudly, his arm slipping around my shoulders. I wriggle uncomfortably, the intensity of Mrs Harrington's features appears razor-sharp in the chandelier's brightness. Her eyes are carved from the harshest blue sapphire that absorbs every inch of me in one easy swoop. "And she's staying for dinner," August adds. I thump him in the ribs, breaking free of his hold. Nudging her husband's head aside, his mom stands tall in a black pantsuit and makes her way over to me.

"Mrs Harrington, I—"

"Please, call me Rebecca." She swipes her hand through the air and I still. A small smile breaches the stiff line of her lips, putting me more on edge than the scowl I thought was permanent. "There's no need to explain. I've seen the surveillance footage. It's clear to me now your actions weren't your own, and at the first sign of trouble, that awful man in the shadows ran off and let you take the blame." Sighing, Mrs Har—Rebecca hangs her head and takes my hand in hers. "I'm not too much of a prude to know that sometimes we do things to please others. Johnny, here is no angel." She smirks at her husband, and he gives me a two-fingered salute.

"Double-rehab attendee." He nods without a trace of regret. Leaning back, he rests his head on one hand, showcasing the sleeve of ink lining his arm. "We all make mistakes, but it's what you do to fix them that counts. Still rocking out, and eleven years sober over here." He holds out his fist and I move forward to fist-bump him.

Nancy calls, informing us that dinner is ready, and everyone shifts towards the door, expecting me to follow. I spin, feeling like I've entered an alternate universe. Johnny draws his son under his arm, scraping his knuckles against August's scalp like a pair of brothers. Rebecca holds back, stretching her hand out towards my shoulder.

"Come. You haven't lived until you've tasted Nancy's risotto." Mimicking her small smile, I step into Rebecca's reach. Soothing her hand over the top of my back, we walk to the dining table, where I see Carl has returned. Unlike before, his black fatigues have been swapped out for a casual t-shirt and jeans, barely stretching over his muscled frame. Amongst the perfectly arranged bowls, cutlery, glasses, and a flourishing bouquet centerpiece, a place has been set for me at August's side. Nancy and Carl are opposite, while the two head's of the household are on either end.

"I never asked if you have any allergies, Candy," Nancy comments, halting her descent into the chair, in case I suddenly disclose that I do. Shaking my head, she grins and reaches over to dish out two large ladles of risotto. The smells reaching me are heavenly, even before my bowl is full. Rebecca remains standing to uncork a bottle of wine, and she pours a glass for herself, Nancy, and Carl. August tips his empty glass her way, nudging me to do the same. I do not.

"Erm, I don't think so, somehow," Rebecca says, retracting the bottle and trying to give her the sternest look. It falls apart at the seams, and she grumbles *'oh, go on then'* whilst pouring a tiny measure for us both. In that instant, I know for a fact, August has his mom wrapped around his little finger. Johnny reclines back in his dining chair, the same way he used the chaise lounge—as if every seat in the house is his throne. Reaching across, Nancy taps his bowl edge, urging him to sit upright with a raised eyebrow.

"What's the use of all those chiropractor appointments if you're not even going to attempt straightening your posture?" She tuts, and I watch the exchange with interest. Rebecca smiles over the rim of her wine glass, not interrupting or bothered by the paid help reprimanding her husband.

"My posture isn't the problem." Johnny rolls his eyes and takes the ladle to serve himself instead. "The endless gigs are."

"No one forces you to body surf the crowd each night," Rebecca comments, blowing on her food. Shrugging one shoulder, Johnny takes his bowl in his hand and slumps back, much to Nancy's disapproval. Sniggering under his breath,

August shifts until his knee knocks against mine, and suddenly, I'm ripped from the sitcom around me and fully aware of my own presence again. Turning my head downwards towards the rich walnut table, I dig into my meal.

"Shall we attend the mall's grand reopening before you head off tomorrow, Nancy?" Rebecca asks, making polite conversation. I crease my eyebrows at August, and he not-so-quietly fills my silent question.

"When my parents are home, Nancy is relieved from caring for me. She pretends to have a beach house in the suburbs, but we all know she doesn't go much further than across the hall." He smirks and Nancy gasps. Holding a hand to her chest dramatically, she hunts for someone to take her side and comes up empty. My eyes slide to Carl, who pointedly ignores the lot of us.

"I do happen to have a lovely house on the coast, for your information," Nancy begins, and Johnny chuckles.

"You don't go back to it though." Johnny points a forkful of risotto at her. "I'm sure Carl would love a mini-break, instead of complaining about the increase of hair clogging his drain." Carl grunts, his bald head bobbing in agreement.

"Some midnight skinny dipping wouldn't go amiss either," Carl grumbles into his bowl and Nancy smacks his shoulder. Their easy banter and the closeness of their chairs occurs to me as I put all the pieces together, and honestly, I don't know how I didn't see it sooner. Johnny's laughter picks up, his hand raising for a solid high-five. August copies, raising his hand too, but his mother pushes it down before Carl can reciprocate.

"You're too young to high-five that," she warns and August puffs out his chest.

"Some would argue I'm more grown up than the supposed man of the house," he retorts, flashing his pearly whites at his father. Johnny pauses, eyeing a piece of his lengthy hair that's dipped into the edge of his bowl. Lifting it between his forefinger and thumb, his hazel eyes flick to Rebecca.

"Don't you dare," she scolds. "We have a guest." Johnny pushes the strands of hair into his mouth, sucking off the risotto residue, and Rebecca pinches the bridge of her nose. "I should have listened to my mother and married that helicopter pilot," she groans, much to our amusement.

"Sounds boring as hell," Johnny snipes back, winking at his wife.

"The pilot would have had better posture though," Nancy agrees with Rebecca. I find myself smiling, thoroughly enjoying the ping pong game of back and forth remarks.

Diving into eating, the conversation fizzles out, other than a few tales from Johnny about his tour. All the while, August is slyly nudging his way closer until his leg is fully pressed against mine and he reaches for my hand beneath the table. I flinch, brushing him off. Catching my eye with a cheeky grin on his face, I mouth that it's time for me to go when August sits bolt upright.

"You know what would be nice," he announces in the middle of Johnny's broken down RV story. "A games night, like we used to when Uncle Merlot would come to visit." I blink rapidly, but the notion moves too quickly for me to process the strange choice in name.

"Ooh!" Nancy shoots upwards, snatching the empty bowls. Carl's still eating from his, but she whips it out from beneath his spoon without caring for his warning growl. "I'll make game snacks! Don't start without me." Disappearing into the kitchen, the clatter of dirty dishes being abandoned in the basin is followed by the clanging of cupboard doors. Rebecca pats her mouth clean with a cloth napkin and pushes to her feet.

"I'd better go rein her in before she uses up the entire food supply." Carl also stands, announcing he needs a smoke if we're going to start 'that UNO reverse shit'. His words, not mine. So that leaves just Johnny, who seems to be drifting into a nap, and August who has managed to wriggle his hand into mine. Clasping his fingers closed, he grins like he's made some big achievement, and I suppose he has.

"Uncle Merlot?" I question quietly. "What kind of name is that?"

"My grandmother was…eccentric." August winks and Johnny chuckles deep in his chest.

"She was a freaking fruit loop, you mean." Cracking an eye at me, Johnny laces his hands over his stomach. "My mother spent the seventies riding such a high, it's a miracle she even realized she popped out two kids. She thought she'd name us after the excuses for their existence. My brother was blamed on the Merlot wine and I…" He rolls his one eye back to sleep.

"She said the johnny broke," August adds with muffled laughter. "It's the nickname for a condom." I gasp, trying to conceal my chuckle behind my hand, but Johnny doesn't seem to mind. I suppose there's a lot to be said for crappy mother's. It speaks volumes that Rebecca would only want the best life for August when there's so many ruined childhood's floating around—although I bet my life August would much prefer it if she were home more often.

"See, Candy." Johnny raises his arms wide, still feigning sleep. "You don't have to be homeless to have a dysfunctional family." August's laughter dies, and like a bullet, Rebecca has spun around the corner and whipped Johnny with a coiled tea towel. Jolting him upright with a yelp, Rebecca's blue eyes shine with the icy chill of an avalanche at her cowering husband.

"Shit, I'm so sorry—that was insensitive of me." Johnny bows his head and Rebecca retreats with a glare.

"It's fine," I rush to say, although the blush coating my cheeks says otherwise. "It's rather comforting, in all honesty." Sharing a lopsided smile with Johnny, I notice August's grip on my hand has clenched twice as tight while Carl strolls back in.

"What did I miss?" he asks, sensing the tension in the air.

"Nothing," Nancy sing-songs from the kitchen. "Set up Monopoly, we'll be right there!" Carl groans, muttering about the choice of game, and I'm starting to think, he just doesn't like games in general.

Rebecca walks past the doorway, juggling a couple of bowls in her hands, and August finally releases my clammy hand.

"Here, Mom. Let me help." I smile after him, catching myself too late when I suddenly notice Johnny is staring at me. In the glimpse of the light, and with the angle of his arms, I spot a few scars poking out from beneath the artwork inked across his forearms.

"It's nice having you here." He nods and I tense up. Prickles tap at the back of my neck, like reality has come knocking, and I rub the sensation away.

"Um, can I use your bathroom?" I duck out of my chair while Johnny relays directions, unknowing I've been in this apartment more than him in the last two weeks. Opting for the one in Nancy's bedroom, I close the door and slump against the wooden door. Every time I start to feel comfortable here, the cold wash of the truth is ready to douse any glimpse of happiness I could allow myself. I came to say goodbye. Not to play happy families, as if I won't be back on the street tomorrow. But then I remind myself for that exact reason, I should enjoy every possible moment.

Splashing my face with cold water, I give myself a pep talk in the mirror. My brown hair is curling just past my shoulders, the sweater I'm wearing grimy and stained. My cheeks are flushed, and my chocolate brown eyes are glistening for once. Giving myself a little smile, I pass back through Nancy's bedroom when voices in the hallway reach me.

"Please, Mom," August begs quietly. "She fits in so well." My eyes widen and I freeze, unable to step out from the shadows.

"August, darling, people don't run away for no reason. Something or someone will be looking for her and…you are my primary concern. I have to keep you safe." There's a pause as I close my eyes, imagining her soothing his lengthy dark hair down the sides of his face. "Besides, you're returning to school, and our next tour starts in a matter of weeks. It's just not feasible."

"But you could take her with you. Then she won't be traceable, and there must be some way she could earn her keep. I really…want to help her, Mom." August sighs in defeat, resigning to the fate I've already accepted.

"I know you do, my sweet boy. I like her, I really do. Let's enjoy tonight, and then I'll reach out to some agencies that will be able to give Candy the best chance at a new start." My eyes fly open. No! No agencies. No law enforcement. They will return me back to my lying foster father, and I know I won't survive him a second time.

Waiting for the pair of shadows to walk past the doorway, I slip out and push my feet back into my boots. Spinning, I bump into August's chest as he merely stands there, his hazel eyes all-knowing.

"I'm really sorry—I just remembered, I have to get going. Thank you for dinner."

"Candy, please—" He tries to grab for me, but I hold my hand up.

"Don't." Smiling sadly, I lean forward and bravely place a kiss on his cheek. "Don't ruin it. Let's leave this on a good note." Without saying another word, I twist the door handle behind me and back away from the boy I could have easily curled up against. To let him soothe my fears and fill me with his false promises. Giving August a small wave, I shoot down the staircase before my feet betray me and run straight back.

"I'll be at the skatepark on Lux and 3rd tomorrow from 11am," August's voice echoes around the halls, catching me just before I manage to escape the building. Dammit, I curse to myself. I really wish he hadn't said that.

Half a Sandwich and a Soggy Packet of Chips

Appearing from a subway station as far from the skatepark as possible, I continue to have the same fight between my heart and my head. It's no good, my heart is too loud, and my self-loathing doubles with every step. I shouldn't have let myself get attached to August and his family, but I feel a tie to them like I've never experienced before. If this is what love is, I understand why it drives people to insanity. Even the barest touch is enough to have me hooked, craving for the next touch, the next hug, just like an addict.

Mulling around the streets, more focused on kicking an empty can than contemplating the loss of my soul, I draw to a halt and look around. I recognize this place. Retracing my steps backwards, despite the grumbles I get from those who bump into me, I come level with an alley. Elation rockets through me like a firework, bursting with the excitement of a familiar face. Or several, as it turns out. Redirecting myself, I stroll towards the elongated tarp tent with a friendly smile at the ready.

"Well, look who it is," Mighty McDwarfy announces, waving

me closer. A long whistle leaves the ghostly white man, his eyes trailing the length of my expensive clothing before settling on my black studded boots. Blushing, I'm welcomed into their fold as easily as the first night with Patrick, dropping down by the pirate.

"So, you haven't become rat food yet?" He nudges me with a smirk and I shake my head.

"Not this one," the hunchback witch replies, shuffling over. "She's made of tougher stuff." Pulling me beneath her arm, she rubs my shoulder in comfort, and I fall into her embrace. A woman I barely know, yet she feels as familiar to me as any foster parent I've had.

Returning to the lunch I seem to have interrupted, the ex-commander reaches over to pass me half a sandwich and an opened packet of crisps. I accept them with a muffled thanks, swallowing the guilt over how well I've been eating lately, whilst they have suffered. Even with the little they have, these people still openly share with me.

Unlike last night's dinner table, there's no casual conversation or easy banter here. Just people lost to their own thoughts, chowing down the only hot meal they might get for a while. I bite into mine, moving the warm tuna mayo and soggy bread around my mouth with my tongue. Tears prick at the back of my eyes, the welcomed feeling becoming tainted with the sinking realization I can't have the best of both worlds.

"Why so quiet, little one?" the friendly witch asks, copying the nickname Patrick would use. It should bother me, but considering I'm rather tall for my age, I like the irony. It's not like I've had a normal childhood with pet names before—unless 'that irritating mistake' counts.

"I'm struggling to find my purpose," I sigh, the weight of the world returning to rest on my shoulders.

"Good luck with that one, kid," the ghost chuckles dryly. "Not even the rich and famous can find their purpose. That's why so many overdose."

"Don't think you can say that in this day and age," the witch reprimands him with a knowing glare. Shrugging, the ghost tosses his trash into his shopping cart, and wipes his hands on a holey vest hanging loosely from his bony shoulders.

"I eat scraps from the trash and live in a cardboard box. I'll say whatever I damn well please." He tilts his head stubbornly, and I huff a laugh.

"Perks of having nothing to lose," I muse out loud, earning myself a small cheer, and a few pats on the back.

"Now you're getting it." The pirate nudges my side. Suddenly everyone edges in closer, as if I just passed another phase of their initiation. The rest of the sandwich doesn't seem to taste as bland and gritty now, and I wash it down with a bottle of warm water. I'm slightly concerned by the yellowish twinge in the liquid, but don't want to actively decline another offered gift. Not when they have so little to give, yet do anyway.

"Come on," G.I Joe announces. Standing to his full height, he stretches out a fully tattooed arm, and I take his hand. Dragging me away, I wave a quick goodbye and struggle to keep up with his long strides. "You're too good for this place." I frown, chewing on my bottom lip. People keep saying that, but how do they know? And, why didn't my foster parents ever feel the same way? I'm starting to think it's because I was the easiest to ignore, but now it's time to start making some.

Leading me into the street, I tug my hand free before anyone gets the wrong idea. There's no way this tanned, tattooed middle-aged man is my dad, and anything else suggested by the questioning eyebrows passing our way makes me shudder.

The sun is still hanging overhead, refusing to set on this

never ending day. It's almost as if the entire universe is forcing me to rethink my decision to ditch August today. Focusing on the pavement beneath my boots, I crash into the back of G.I Joe when he suddenly stops.

"Steady on," he mumbles, setting me firmly on my feet. Peering around his side, I see the queue of people lining the sidewalk up to a five storey building made of brick and misery. Even without the long line of ripped clothing, matted hair, and intense body odor drifting my way, there's nothing welcoming about a bland building that looms over the city. Blacked out windows and a non-descript shutter blocks our view of what's inside—although I can guess.

"This is the Street Angels hostel, isn't it?" I ask G.I Joe. He grunts and nods, pushing me into line and taking a step back himself. Opening his mouth to respond, he decides against it and settles for nudging my chin aside with his fist. Then he's gone. I get it—army dude that can't do goodbyes. No doubt he's seen horrors others can't even imagine, and lost more than I've ever had.

Finding myself alone, I push my hands into my tracksuit pockets and rock back and forth on my boot heels. My hand closes around the last stick of gum I have, and now's as good a time as any to enjoy it.

Chew. Pop. Chew. Pop. I sway and tap my feet for what must be over an hour, all the while popping my gum. The woman in front tuts at me multiple times, not that I care, until she whips around and reveals the bundle hidden in a sling across her front. Popping my last bubble, I retract the gum back into my mouth and avoid her gaze. When she doesn't turn away, I glance upwards to see her sharp eyes hovering over my shoulder.

"They friends of yours?" she asks, and I follow her gaze. A group of men dressed all in black are hanging back, ducking into the line when I notice them. After a minute, one sticks his head out to see if I'm still watching and shifts out of view again. Weird. My thoughts drift back to the Drive-In, but since I was unable to get a clear view of their faces in the dark, I can't tell if these are the same men.

Sharing a look with the woman I was sure wanted to smack the annoying out of me a moment ago, she jerks her head for me to jump the queue and stand in front of her. I manage to skip further along by faking a retch, threatening to hurl all over anyone still in my way. By the time I've neared the front of the line, and poked my head through the mass of heads scowling at me, I spot the men, who are now trying to barge their way past the woman with the baby. Yep. They are definitely following me.

At my back, the shutter flaps open and the crowd surge forward, catching me off guard. Losing my footing, I scramble out of the way as starving women shout and scared toddlers cry. Crawling on my hands and knees, I somehow find myself at the back of the building, and temporarily hidden from view. Then, I run.

Skidding through a muddy zone between the brick wall and a metal fence, I wriggle myself through a gap only big enough for a supermodel. Or, a starved homeless girl with more bone than muscle. Hopping down from a mini ledge, my boots land heavily in the delivery bay. The same Street Angels van that visited the alley is there, being stocked up on fresh produce for another round of meals on wheels. Those carrying bags question my presence as I slip by, evading the few hands that try to stop me. Not a chance when there's men close by who seem to have an interest in me, and this time, I don't have Carl to save my ass.

More shouts come as I rejoin the main street, but this time it's not from the charity workers. Without waiting around, I shove tax-paying citizens out of the way, my heart diving into my throat and hindering my breathing. Gripping the stitch that appears in my side, I refuse to slow.

Flying across busy roads, with some higher power seeing me over unscathed, I spot a darkened area and head directly towards it.

Coming to a halt before a dead end, a hole in the fence at the end of an alley presents my escape. Slithering through, my new clothes tear on the spokes, but I press on. No time to worry about that now. Especially not when a sturdy man's boot stomps down on my hand, drawing a pained cry from my lips. Grinding his heel down, I shove at his ankle uselessly, fighting to pry my hand back, but I can't until he permits it.

Fear grips me as more shoes appear around me, and my exit back through the fence is blocked by a man's hands clutching at my sweater. Yanking me to my feet, the man who has probably broken my fingers leers in my face. He doesn't try to conceal his appearance—middle-aged, clean cut and well-practiced in the art of scowling. He has one of those faces you could slap, and so I do. I have to use my good hand, which happens to be the left, so it has no effect other than to piss him off.

"You'll have to do better than that, Princess." He bares his golden teeth. A whimper escapes me as I recoil into myself, protecting my throbbing hand against my chest.

"Wh-what do you want?" I try to sound confident, but have all the gusto of a wounded puppy. Instead of answering, the man's wide grin is all I see as a bag is pulled over my head from behind, my world going black. I sob, shaking like a leaf but unable to bring myself to fight back. What would I do anyway? With a hand as useless as I am, I merely let the scary man pick me up and carry me off with one saying floating around my mind. Once a victim, always a victim.

"Well, that was anticlimactic," a man from behind grumbles.

"Thought she'd have been more fun to toy with than that." My head flops around next to a firm chest, a sigh being drawn from my lungs. Well, at least my pathetic-ness can contribute to not giving one of these assholes what they want. A decent fight. The others fall into some mumbled chatter while I succumb to a feeling I know all too well. Emptiness. If I were to have a superpower, it'd be detaching my mental from my physical being. I'm halfway through wondering what kind of logo that type of ability would have on my cape when a loud thud sounds.

"What the fuck?!" someone shouts, followed by a series of yells and grunts. I shift my head around, as if that'd help me find the direction of the noises while this hessian bag keeps me fully disorientated. More thuds sound, from what I would imagine are bodies hitting the concrete, and suddenly, I'm tumbling down with them.

Searing pain skates up my back, but I grab the hood off, needing to make sure I don't get stomped on again. Peering up at the bulky shadow standing over me, a familiar voice has both elation and alarm bells flaring inside my mind.

"Always causing trouble, huh, little one?" Patrick smirks. Bending down, he checks me over for injuries and settles on carefully taking my hand in his. "It's okay. I'm just going to look." Giving him full control, Patrick turns my hand over a few times, before setting his dark eyes on me. Then he jerks his wrist suddenly and snaps one of my fingers back into place.

"Jesus Christ!" I shout, tugging my hand away to roll around in pain. Tingles, like a thousand needles penetrating my bloodstream, shoot down the length of my arm, drawing a rogue tear from my eye. Swiping it away with my shoulder, I manage to bring myself to sit upright and breathe slowly, as Patricks watches in amusement.

"Let's get you somewhere safe." He nods, not seeming bothered by the men lying all around us. I frown at their still frames, wondering how Patrick knocked them all out so easily, when he grabs for something black and shiny on the ground. A gun. I swallow thickly, noting how the end of the barrel has a long cylinder attached, like I've seen in movies. Quickly tucking it into the lining of his many coats, Patrick tugs me to my feet and ushers me out of the alley as I try to look back.

"Wait. Are they…?"

"Safety first, questions later," he states, in a tone that contradicts everything he just said.

Selena; My Stripper from Another Flipper

Turns out, Patrick's idea of safety is the very last place I would have wanted to be. The Thirsty Kirsty's doorstop. Taking me around the back this time, he raps his knuckles on the metal fire escape, where a grate in the door is promptly whipped open. The squinted eyes on the other side say nothing, permitting Patrick immediate entry.

"Thanks, Mick," he drawls, striding in while I rush to keep close. A beaded curtain separating the darkened corridors from the main club permits Patrick entry, and then smacks me in the face. Shooing them away, my eyes have barely adjusted to the roaming colored lights circling the stage when a hand grabs my wrist.

"What is she doing back here?" my mom hisses, talking over me to Patrick's back. He spears her a glance, mirth visible in his features, as if life is nothing but one big game to him.

"We ran into some trouble. Candy needs somewhere to hide out while I run an errand." I tense up, only just finding out Patrick plans on leaving me here. Intro music announces a new act on stage, and the cheering crowd becomes too loud to hear. Unlike last time when I visited during the day, the sun has set outside, and the vultures have swarmed in for their pound of flesh.

Tugging on my wrist, my mom drags me away as Patrick calls that he'll be back soon. And then he's gone. I didn't expect some mushy goodbye, but he strides through the drunks and disappears without a look back.

Retreating back into the dark corridor I recently emerged from, the woman who bears so much resemblance to me doesn't acknowledge my presence once. Just keeps tugging me forward until I spy the side of the stage, and the woman dropping into the splits upon it. Glittery red heels are strapped to her feet, and a pair of love heart tassels cover her nipples. That's it. I'm thankful I can't see in between her open legs from this angle as I'm shoved into a cramped room backstage, filled with metal racks and more sequins than I've ever seen.

Releasing me to close the door, my mom steadies her palms on the wood and exhales heavily. When she turns her chocolate eyes in my direction, all I can see is distaste. I've been looked at with this expression before, but by my own flesh and blood? That cuts so much deeper. The small shake of her head and pursed lips scream 'I told you so', without muttering so much as one word.

"So, Candy, huh?" She says, and I realize she didn't hang around long enough the first time to catch my name.

"That's right. Candy Crystal." I raise my chin, owning the name I procured for myself. Not some traditional crap a court document says. My mom huffs a laugh through her nose, assessing me up and down.

"Sounds like you're already on your way to joining the family business." I scrunch up my nose and pull my top lip back in a snarl. No freaking way. It's my turn to look her up and down like yesterday's trash. "Oh, don't look at me like that," my mom hisses defensively. "Our bodies are our best assets. The money is good, and you won't have inhibitions holding you back your entire life."

"You can believe whatever skewed version of reality you like," I reply, sounding like the real adult here. "I refuse to ever step foot on that stage. My body, my terms. Not for someone to take with their eyes, hands, or otherwise." Snorting, my mom tells me to suit myself and barges past, diving into the racks of clothing.

"Either way, you'll need a disguise now they know your face," she finally says, slicing through the tension between us with a blood-coated blade. Notice she didn't specify who *they* are, keeping me in the dark like usual. Trying and failing to find anything marginally acceptable, she sighs and moves towards the sewing machine to hold up cut offs, as if she'll patch them all back together. I watch the scene play out as if I'm a spare part, just standing by the wall as my life is taken out of my control once again.

"Why didn't you want me?" I ask, unable to keep the question inside. I've always told myself I don't care either way. That I was probably lucky because my birth mother was worse than any predicament I've found myself in. Yet, here she is—healthy, sober, alive. The opposite of what I was expecting all these years. Her hand freezes over a hanger, a visible shudder slithering down her spine.

"I had no choice." Tilting her chin my way, I note the similarity in our face shapes and instantly despise it. I don't want to be anything like the coward I see before me.

"Nice cop out," I nod slowly. Spinning with a come-back on

the edge of her tongue, the door suddenly whips open, concealing me behind it.

"Art's looking for you," a female voice says. "And he's pissed." Sighing, my mom's eyes flick to me and back again.

"Selena, I need a favour. I'll give you half of my tips for the rest of the week," she bargains, and I wait out the pause that follows.

"All of your tips for the weekend."

"Deal," my mom groans, nudging the door for me to step away from the wall. "This is Candy. She needs a makeover—an unrecognisable one. Will you find something *appropriate* for her to wear?" Selena rounds the door, her red lips turning up into a full smile.

"What a beautifully blank canvas," she grins. I recognize her as the girl I saw on the stage during my first visit. Long brunette hair floats down her back, her boobs held up in a tiny crop top that seems to display her nipples more than if she were naked. Her killer abs impress me as much now as they did then, and a pair of hot pants just about cover her ass.

"Um, thanks, I guess." I frown. A sharp bark sounds from further down the hall, and my mom jolts into action—I suppose the man bellowing is looking for her. Looking at the rack again, I sigh and tap my foot as I'm left to Selena's mercy.

"Come with me. I've got a much better idea than these gimmicky costumes." Exiting the room behind her, the ball of anxiety in my chest lessens with every step I take away from the stage area. A small staircase takes us down to a lower level, this one nothing like those put on for show. No fancy wallpaper or plush wood flooring. Selena's heels click on the exposed concrete flooring, and the door she leads me to is nondescript and dark. Yet inside, a burst of pink raises my eyebrows to my hairline.

"Ta da!" Selena beams, holding out her arms wide. "I don't get visitors here, like ever. This is my personal space." I glance from the fluffy bed covers and cushions, to the posters of topless men, and a naked fireman's calendar on the wall. Every inch of the walls beneath are baby pink, including the fake shaggy rug running the length of the floor. Beneath the vanity with a huge spotlight mirror is a mini fridge, filled with snacks I didn't think someone as skinny as Selena would eat.

"You…live here? Under the club?" I ask, stepping inside. Kicking off her heels, she drops onto the bed with a bounce.

"We all do. Except your mom, who gets a nice little apartment up top to herself. She's Art's favorite."

"And Art would be…"

"Oh, sorry, I thought you knew. Art is the club's owner. He recruited me fresh out of college. It's not a bad job and the tips are good, but his contract is iron-clad. The dancers must live here and we don't get paid essentially. More like, we ask for whatever we want and Art will see to it. I saved up once for a spa weekend, but then the other dancers conveniently got food poisoning and I had to work instead. Next time though. " She tips her head side to side. Stretching out her long legs, Selena waits for me to tentatively lower myself onto the edge of the mattress.

"So…a makeover?" I change the subject, not wanting to get into whatever cult is happening here. "There's some men…" I trail off, realizing the threats against me are currently lying face-down in some alley, but something my mom said gives me pause. *They* know my face. Whoever *'they'* may be.

"Say no more. We're all hiding from some asshole that ruined us." Leaning forward, Selena pulls a fabric drawer out from beneath her bed and I shift my legs aside. "But my motto is: why hide what you can flaunt. So, what do you say?"

Reaching down, Selena plucks out two boxes of hair dye. One, a bleach whitener, and the other, a vibrant pink. My eyes are as wide as dinner plates as I look from the smiling model on the box to the stripper opposite, a crazed expression settling over her face.

It's moments like these when I can tell my decision will alter the course of my life. Not just something as simple as a hair color, but the persona that comes with it. If I accept the challenge in Selena's eyes, I won't just be some homeless girl. I'll be the feisty street rat everyone knows. The one who can't fade into the background. So my only option will be to stand up and fight. What did Patrick say? We've got to make some noise to remind the world what it forgot. Well…I've been pushed around, put down, and as of late, hunted for some unknown reason. I'd say it's time I showed everyone I'm not going away quietly. I deserve a fresh start, and through the skin of my teeth, I'm going to damn well have it.

As soon as my head shifts into a steady nod, the decision flares into the best idea I've ever had. Soon, I'm bobbing up and down as Selena claps her hands, and directs me towards her vanity stool. Brushing the lengths of my hair, she pushes an iPod into its docking station and fills the room with the latest R&B jams.

"Help yourself to the gummy bears," Selena tells me, pushing an open packet across the desk towards me. I do just that, as she sections my hair and proceeds to coat it in thick layers of white slush. Picking up a reddish gummy bear, I hold him between my forefinger and thumb, speaking to the squishy face with my mind.

Take a good look, buddy. This is the last time anyone will see me as a poor little orphan girl. Then I pop him in my mouth and chew with a wide smile.

The hair dryer turns off, and my ankles knock together in excitement. The towel covering the mirror hinders me from seeing my reflection prematurely. While we'd been waiting for the dye to set, Selena painted my face with her masses of make-up, and we'd found an old outfit in her wardrobe that would fit me. A pair of black PVC trousers with a silver chain linking two of the belt loops together. On top, a cropped white t-shirt with a pink love heart in the centre makes my chest look bigger than it actually is .

"Is she done yet?" a giddy voice asks from behind the door, followed by hushed whispers. We'd caught the attention of the other girls when we'd ventured into the communal showers, my bright pink dye discoloring the water by everyone's feet and swirling into the drain.

"Oh, she's ready," Selena muses, flicking my hair over my shoulders. It feels incredibly soft, like feathers brushing over the back of my neck. The crowd of girls burst into the room as Selena whips the towel off the mirror and we all freeze in surprise. Woah. Fuschia pink waves frame my painted face, my lashes fully extended over my chocolate brown eyes, and my freckles enhanced. The arch of my eyebrows has been perfected and any stray hairs plucked away. If I were being truthful, the make-up is slightly too heavy for me, but I can't deny that I look at least five years older, and…beautiful.

"What's all the commotion about?" a male says, and instantly, the girls disappear like they were never here.

Stepping aside, Selena's hand rests on my shoulder as a man strides closer in the mirror's reflection. A pompous man in a white suit and cowboy hair approaches, his round gut swaying with each step of his cowboy boots.

"Well, who does this happen to be?" he grins in a creepy, predatory kind of way. I shrink until I remember—I'm not that girl anymore. I'm going to own my new look and bite back at those who question it.

"Meet Candy. The girl whose name is as sweet as her appearance." Selena beams, still running her hands through my silky locks. The transformation I've been through in the past two weeks, both physically and mentality, will ensure no one from my old life will recognise me. "Candy, this is Art." I look him over again, a bitter taste filling my mouth. So, this is the man who brings girls here and retains their hard-earned money. I at least expected someone handsome who could lure people in with his charm, but there's nothing appealing about the man looming over me. Quite the opposite.

"Very nice job, Selena," Art praises, reaching over to touch my hair, but I'm too fast. Shooting to my feet, I spin and cross my arms, drawing his attention to my small chest. My snarled lip and popped hip only seems to please him more. "She'll make a great addition to the team." A retort halts on the end of my tongue, my perfectly prepped eyebrows shooting upwards.

"You set me up?!" I shout at Selena, and she doesn't even have the decency to look embarrassed.

"Sorry, Doll, it's in your blood. Better off accepting it now," she shrugs, and any warm, sisterly vibes I was getting from her dissipate. Is there no one honest left in this world? My mind trails to August, but I shove those thoughts away, focusing on how I will never accept that selling my body is in my blood. Never.

"Doesn't matter either way. I'm thirteen," I scoff, my teeth clenching tightly.

"Don't worry about that." Art swipes his hands through the air. "You can earn your stay bussing tables until you're mature enough." I note that he says 'mature enough', rather than referring to a legal age, and in that instant, I decide I hate him. I hate every bone in his body, and every disgustingly, dirty thought that passes through his mind.

"Firstly, there's nothing you can offer to get me to stay here. And secondly, you'll never get me on that stage." I scowl at Selena for the role she played in preparing me for Art's approval, and I move to stride past him.

"We'll see," he challenges, and I growl low in my chest, not faltering in my footsteps.

"No, we will not," a voice that isn't mine agrees. My mom steps into sight just as I crash into her. Grabbing me by the arms, the surprise in her gaze is undeniable, followed by another disapproving sigh. Tucking me aside, she tilts her chin defiantly at her owner. I mean, employer. "Candy isn't staying," she states coldly. It's clear my presence is grating on her, and I reckon the new version of me would choose to stay for that reason alone. Yet, that will send the wrong message to those cheering and stomping on the floor overhead. I am not, nor will I ever be, for sale.

"You of all people should know, I always get what I want." Art chuckles to himself. That's all I need to have my feet moving back towards the staircase. I'll take strangers chasing me in the dark any day over a self-righteous prick who thinks I'll make a career out of getting naked for him and his clientèle.

My mom says something about being serious this time, but I don't care anymore, the music of the upper level envelopes around me as I ascend the stairs. Passing the back of the stage, a show is in full swing now with three performers dancing in unison. I only take one wrong turn looking for the back door, and by the time Mick is opening it for me, my mom is there to see me out.

"I was expecting something a little more subtle. " She eyes my hair with clear distaste. Good, I like it even better now.

"Then maybe you should have raised me to meet your preferences." I cock an eyebrow, stepping out into the cool night air. The temperature has dropped and I can smell a storm on the way, but I won't be cowering back inside or asking for a jacket. The new me will work that out when the rain starts. Grabbing onto my bicep, my mom whips me around, her face a breath away from mine.

"Life isn't as simple as your tiny mind would like to believe," she grits out, keeping her voice low. I imagine she doesn't want Mick to hear, since he's the only one nearby, but I don't keep my voice down. Instead, I shout at the top of my lungs.

"Do I look like life has been simple?!" I rip my arm from her grip and raise them out wide. "Do you really think I'd be here with you right now if I'd been raised on a bed of love and nurturing?" The fight escapes her in a pained sigh. So much going unsaid between us as a well-known shadow strolls closer, clutching at the backpack on his shoulder.

"Is Candy ready yet?" Patrick asks my mom, sparing a glance my way and then doing a double take beneath the street lamp. "Oh, holy shit. I mean, holy wow. You look freaking awesome. Sorry, my job took longer than I expected. But I've got you something." I blink a few times, watching his hand disappear into his mass of jackets.

"I'll leave you to it," my mom says, retreating inside, but my attention is on the long object being pulled out and handed to me. Smooth in my palms, I rotate the bat in my hands, in awe at the shade of pink coating the outside.

"Lucky guess on my part," Patrick chuckles, flicking my hair over my shoulder. "I thought you could do with a weapon of your own. Tomorrow, I'll teach you how to use it."

"On someone's head?" I ask, suddenly worried I might be

pushed further than my new ballsy attitude was prepared to go so soon.

"What do you think I am?!" Patrick puts his hand on his chest, feigning innocence. "No, at the batting cages. Obviously." I grin, holding the bat to my chest as if it were a pet. Even better, it's my first ever gift. A thoughtful one at that, so as I trail behind Patrick, I know I've made the right choice. I'm finally where I should be.

Look At All These ♥ Chickens

It's official. The batting cages are my new favorite place to be. The burn on my muscles. The rush of cracking a baseball as far as possible. Even the times I missed, laughter streamed from my lips between bubbles of chewing gum.

Spying Patrick over by the hot dog stand, charming the full-bellied guy while robbing him blind every time he serves a customer, I drop down beside my backpack. I was surprised Patrick had been thoughtful enough to fetch it for me, and thankful I don't have to return to Swish Street to get it myself.

Unzipping the main compartment, I pull out a navy sweater with a super soft lining that smells distinctly like August. This wasn't one of the purchases Nancy made for me, and I can't say I mind. Unfolding the arms, I spot a loose piece of paper tucked into the neckline. A group of girls walk by then and I crush the sweater to my chest, not wanting anyone to see. Whatever is hiding in there, I'm sure it's not by accident, and that means it's meant for me.

Once the coast is clear, I investigate further. I discover that it's not just any piece of paper, but a ticket for the zoo. The date is circled in blue pen, and just so there's no confusion, August's handwriting beneath tells me to meet him at the entrance at 1PM.

Counting on my fingers, from the last time I knew what day it was, I realize this ticket is for today, and he's requested I meet him within the hour. Dammit.

Pulling the sweater on, I clench my arms over my knotted stomach and rock on my heels, the ticket concealed in my hand. Digging my teeth into my bottom lip, I watch Patrick stride back over with a hot dog in both hands.

"Lunch is on me." He grins and I roll my eyes. Technically, it's on the poor sap who doesn't realize his profits will be down today. Tucking the ticket into my back pocket, I accept the hot dog and nibble at it, my mind reeling. I shouldn't go. I shouldn't want to go. But a day out at the zoo, and a day with August… those are two things I can't pass up. So now, all that's left is to think of a convincing lie to tell Patrick. Why I can't go with the truth is beyond me, but I just know it's not a wise idea.

"So this afternoon," Patrick interrupts my lie-invention progress. "I've got a few jobs to run again. Ones you can't tag along for. Think you'll be able to keep yourself entertained for a while?" Fighting to show the relief washing over me, I nod and shrug.

"Yeah, no problem," I settle for, in a rush to finish my hot dog now. Patrick watches me carefully while I avoid his gaze, rubbing my mouth on the back of my sleeve. Slipping the bag strap over my shoulder, I stand and stretch my back out. "Well I'm gonna head for a walk. See where the day takes me. Shall I meet you back around here later, or…" I trail off, trying to not seem like I'm in a rush to get away.

"I'm sure I'll find you around. I taught you everything you know, remember." Patrick stands and pats me on the shoulder, muttering something under his breath.

"Say again?" I ask, but he's already wandering away at a casual pace. Shrugging, I shoot off in the opposite direction to hail the first cab that'll take me. The cabbie gives me a few curious glances, which I put down to my fabulous new hair, and we sit in silence the whole way to the zoo.

Bang on 1PM, we pull up on the sidewalk and a beaming August casually leans through the window to pay the driver. Stepping out of the back, I wait patiently, clasping my hands in front of me, waiting for him to turn around.

"You came!" August suddenly whips me into a tight hug, trapping my arms between us. Giving me a shake, he puts me back on my feet and steps back to assess my new look. My hair is swept back behind my ears, my body hidden in his baggy sweater and a pair of gray sports leggings. Still, my trusty leather boots are snuggly on my feet. My most prized possession, never failing to suit any outfit.

"Do you…like it?" I ask, losing all confidence in my bold choice. Those hazel eyes roam my hair, my clothes, and return to my face with an unusual glint.

"You look incredible." He exhales, as if I've left him breathless, and I look around for a reason to change the subject.

"Where's Carl?" I ask, not spotting the bald headed male who isn't usually too far behind. August smirks, pushing his tongue into his cheek.

"He managed to convince Nancy to take that trip to her beach house." I raise an eyebrow, still not convinced he's actually across the other side of the city on his own. Rolling his hazel eyes and reading my mind, August chuckles under his breath. "My dad will be sleeping mostly until his next tour. It's harder for him to resist the temptation of drink or drugs when he's bored, so he prefers to sleep. And my mom had to attend a business meeting. So, naturally, I'm safe inside my room with a textbook in my hands."

"I feel like I'm a bad influence on you." I tut.

"Nah, I just have an excuse to leave the house now, rather than sit around obeying orders." He winks. I chew on my lip again, not knowing if that's better or worse. I should demand he goes back home to study like a good boy. But he's here now, and it seems a shame to waste one of the last days of summer we'll get this year.

Ducking my head, August's fingers on my chin lifts my face back up to his. "I really am so glad you came."

Placing a feather-light kiss on my cheek, his hand slips into mine and he leads me towards the zoo's entrance. Buying us two tickets, words are exchanged with the booth attendant, but I can't hear them. I'm too busy trying to come back down from the high that's gripping me, my heart expanding across the entirety of my chest, and my feet shuffling forward of their own accord.

"I've booked us onto the safari, if that's okay with you?" August says from beside me, his fingers still linked in mine. Passing beneath the arched entrance banner, the path splits four-ways to follow named signs to different 'regions'.

"Uh huh," I answer weakly. Happy to take the lead, August diverts left towards the *African Pridelands*, never once tugging or rushing me. Carefully planted trees cover the enclosures and provide much needed shade, so we can't foresee what's around each corner. Rounding a long pane of glass nestled between the foliage, a lion roars on the other side and I flinch. His mane is to die for, large and incredibly thick like the model for a shampoo commercial. Brushing the length of his golden body against the glass, he meanders towards a crowd of lionesses waiting on a raised log podium. All the while, August is laughing his ass off at my tight grip on his hand.

"Shut up." I nudge him playfully. "I just didn't, like, expect it to actually be real." This makes him and a few others nearby laugh harder, and even I can hear my own stupidity.

"What were you expecting? Cardboard cutouts?" August rasps, clutching his side.

"No, you baboon." I chuckle and pretend to tug my hand away. Luckily, he doesn't let me. "I've just never seen an exotic animal before." The enclosure is much bigger than I was expecting, my mind having conjured tiny cages and smelly conditions. The lions have masses of land just to the four of them, perfectly configured to have as much greenery as boulders to climb, and even their own stream. We stand there until the lionesses have stretched out, yawned, and fallen back to sleep beside their king.

Only when I'm ready does August move on, listing facts about the animals we see next. Meerkats, a crested porcupine, sulcata tortoises, and many, many monkeys. He's been here before. That much is clear. Everyone else is holding paper maps, trying to navigate the winding paths, while he is strolling through with confidence.

Descending a narrow set of stone steps, we cut through to a dirt track where a jeep is waiting. The sides are missing and a zebra pattern has been painted across the body. The driver puts away his newspaper and waves us over with a warm smile.

"After you." August helps me into the back seat and follows in right after. We wait a few moments for another visitor to join —a woman in her fifties with a huge straw hat. The leopard print of her dress fits with the surrounding and there's a camera clutched in her hands.

"Looks like we're all here," the driver smiles, revving the engine. Easing us through a canopy of trees, we break free of the shade and the breath is stolen from my lungs. Fields of rolling green span in front of us. The track can be seen circling the fields in the distance, and another jeep is mirroring us on the opposite side. Approaching a gate, an attendant quickly slips their phone away to give a formal 'Welcome to the Safari' introduction. Opening the gate, he waves us through, and I peer over my shoulder to watch him secure it shut again.

"Don't worry," August whispers in my ear. "You're completely safe." I smile at him, lowering my head onto his shoulder. Yeah, with him at my side, I know I am. Easing us slowly along the dirt track, a herd of antelope dart in front of the jeep. The driver doesn't panic, maintaining his smooth speed while I marvel at the sight. Flashes of brown and white, rows of curved antlers leaping in unison over a ditch in the road. They're more graceful than I expected, springing on tiny hooves until I'm distracted by the next mammals stomping forward. A huge elephant, with ears flapping and his trunk swaying, follows the antelope's path. This time, the jeep does stop so we can gawk at the sight.

"Wow! How stunning!" The woman up front clicks her camera in every position possible. I snort a laugh when she leans right over the driver, her ass lifting high in the air. With all the subtleness of a sledgehammer, the elephant pauses by our side to trumpet from the bottom of his lungs. August's arms wrap around me as I jolt, drawing me into his hold with a soft chuckle. It's become far too easy to fall into his touch, to depend on him to look after me.

The jeep tour takes an hour to complete, and by then my list of incredible experiences has quadrupled. I've seen a hippopotamus wallowing in a pool of mud, a group of wildebeest stampeding past a rhino, and been spied on by a leopard hiding in the tall grass. To be fair, the list was only formulated when I stepped foot in this zoo and it'll take something incredible to top this.

With the sun shining, and a boy's hands on my waist, I'm in heaven. Returning to the shaded spot where we started, I ease out of the cab a new person. More so than with my hair, this makeover is internal, and I know somehow, someway, I'm going to be okay. Life will work out, and not in any of the ways I expected.

"Shall we grab a bite to eat? I have a special surprise for you after," August tells me. I eye him suspiciously as we take a side path up a steep hill, nudging aside the overgrown bushes. Hiking up to a concrete ledge, we approach a café on a beautiful veranda, overlooking the safari panes below. August tells me to choose one of the outside tables while he grabs us some food. A striped umbrella covers the white plastic, giving us a reprieve from the heat when August returns, a tray in his hands.

"Choose whichever you like, I'll have the other." I grin at the ice cream sundaes, opting for the mint choc chip with chocolate sauce and extra sprinkles.

"I don't expect you to do things for me all the time," I tell him, lifting a heaped spoonful into my mouth. August accepts his own sundae, strawberry with biscuits pieces crumbled on the top.

"I want to," he half-shrugs. "That's what I like about you. No expectations. I've never felt like you were using me for my money, which trust me—many people do. It's the only reason I have any friends at boarding school. Right up until they realize I'm not some meal ticket, and then seem to move onto the next rich kid."

"Isn't everyone at your boarding school rich?" I ask, genuinely curious. August smiles, shuttling his chair closer.

"Not everyone. There's the scholarship students, and then some state grants and special programmes to get more kids in school. Maybe there could—"

"Mmmm," I interrupt that train of thought. "I don't think that's the path for me. But thanks, as always." I smile and peer at him beneath my lashes. Thankfully, August drops the subject and we peer over the balcony at a group of zebras getting randy.

"Besides, if it makes you feel any better." August nudges me. "It's not my money I'm spending, and my parents owe me some companionship points." Finishing off my ice cream sundae, I sit back into his side and exhale. Despite everything he's had handed to him on a silver platter, August hasn't lost his ability to remain humble. I resonate with the lingering sadness stuck behind his hazel eyes. You don't have to be poor to be lonely, and that's why I believe August has been so accepting of me.

Time passes as easily as the afternoon breeze, our sights drifting between the incredible animals below. Trapped, but free at the same time. Whether the springing antelope or racing zebras know they are prohibited by fences or not, they're together and happy. Fed, looked after, and loved by all those who come to marvel at them.

"Ready to go?" August asks after a while, breaking through the serenity cocooned around us. Looking up at him, I find our faces are closer than expected, his breath brushing against my cheek. Nodding, my eyes dip to his lips, and I move in order to hide my blush.

Leading me back towards the real pathway, we don't walk more than five minutes before approaching a lengthy bridge connecting us to a single island. I slow, unsure of the sturdiness of the bridge, despite the thick metal rods holding it in place, but then I see the main attraction.

"Here for the giraffe feeding?" A woman in a green polo shirt and hat with the zoo's logo approached us. My eyes flick to August's, my mouth dropping. Separating from the herd of around ten others, a giraffe, ten times bigger than I expected, strides closer and sticks his chunky head over the edge of the bridge.

"We…us, out there?" I ask, pointing with my index finger. August chuckles, wrapping an arm around my shoulder to draw me closer.

"I'll be with you every step of the way," he promises. The woman hands us a bag of pellets and gives a quick run through on what not to do. Breathing deeply, my eyes widen as I step onto the bridge, finding it much sturdier than I expected. Not that I thought August would book us into the rickety bridge experience, where we run the real risk of falling to our deaths, but still.

Edging towards the bulky head, the giraffe blinks a large eye in my direction. Flicking out his extra long tongue, I shrink back into August's chest.

"It's black!" I gasp. "Why's his tongue black? And that long?!" Muttering words of encouragement into my ear, August reassures me it's perfectly normal and places a pellet into my hand.

"Remember, hold it steady in your finger and thumb. Don't get too close or he might headbutt you."

"Really not helping," I groan, holding out the pellet with a shaky hand. Reaching around, August's hand closes around mine to hold me steady as the orange and brown head veers closer. Slipping his huge tongue out, he coils the pellet into his mouth and I sigh in relief. "Well, that wasn't too—"

Whoosh. Rearing his head back, the giraffe sneezes, slamming a layer of slime all over me and August. The bag of pellets drops from August's hand, raining through the bridge's slats like a waterfall of treats that distracts our leggy friend. I stand stock still, frozen until August's chest against my back begins to judder.

"I'm so sorry," he says, unable to hold back his laughter. I join him, chortling while wiping the slime off my face with the sleeves of his sweater.

"Seriously," I manage to slip out amongst my hysterics. "This has been the best day ever." We slink back to the woman, who has a roll of tissues at the ready. Obviously, this particular giraffe has a knack for soaking his feeders, which might be why they leave the job for naïve members of the public. Clumps of mucus have welded into my pink hair, yet I couldn't care less. I proudly stride around with my sticky hand clasped in August's until we manage to find the restrooms and wash up properly.

"I'd better think about getting back soon," August tells me as we hit the lemur sanctuary. The giant rodents are running overhead, their curled hands gripping the provided ropes with ease and striped tails swishing side to side. Twisting my lips, I nod in understanding. Nothing good can last forever, but I want to hold onto this moment as long as possible. Drawing August into an alcove where the lemurs hide and stash their given pieces of fruit.

"I meant what I said," I tiptoe to put my arms around his shoulders. "This has been the best day I've ever had."

"Same here," he grins, taking the cues of my body to tip his head downwards. Our lips brush with the faintest touch that shoots through me with the electricity of a lightning bolt. His hands splay on the bottom of my back, gently holding me against him, but never forcing. I press my lips harder, wanting to drink in August's very essence. The purity with which he views the world, unhindered by his wealth, or those who have used him for it. Releasing his mouth, I drop my head onto August's shoulder and just stand there, reveling in him. Committing every sensation he brings to the surface into my memory, for when we step out of this hidden cove. All too soon, the attendant calls for last admittance into the caged lemur sanctuary, and we have to step back into reality.

"Shall we hit the gift shop before we go?" August asks, not waiting for a reply. I prefer to wait outside, not wanting to leer over August's shoulder as he promises to be right back. His floppy dark hair blows wildly as he passes under the air conditioning vent at the exit, bounding up to me with a paper bag in his hand. "For you," August insists, and I tut. When I don't immediately take it, he pulls a framed photograph from the bag and flashes it at me. Between the boldly patterned border, the image forces a blurt of laughter from my throat. Caught at the precise moment the giraffe sneezed, the photograph shows August and I flinching away from the snot flying through the air, our faces contorted in disgust.

"I didn't even know there was a camera point there!" I smack his shoulder, holding the photograph close to my chest. A moment I don't need to commit to memory, because I get to keep it forever. Next he pulls out a giraffe teddy bear, snuggling it into my neck with a shy grin.

"I wish I could give you the world," August mumbles, but I won't let the smile on my face shrink.

"I don't need it. This moment is everything." Staring into each other's eyes, a connection solidifies. We might not have forever, or even next week, but we have now. And that's a feeling I'll hold onto the next time the night feels a little too dark. Tucking my souvenirs safely back in the bag, we return to the side of the road where I spot a black BMW waiting over the road. August's dad, Johnny, is sitting behind the wheel, beckoning us over with two tattooed fingers and a bored expression on his face.

"Oops," August says. "Busted." We share a smile, not feeling an ounce of regret when a vehicle skids alongside the sidewalk where we're standing. A man I vaguely recognize hops out of the rear door, grabbing a fistful of August's hair. A shiny object in his hand jutting into my friend's stomach, causing my own to plummet.

"Get in or I shoot," the man growls at me, and without even thinking I dive into the back of the car. Whatever it takes to ensure August's safety. Yet, instead of releasing him, the man shoves August in behind me and ducks his way in too. The gun remains hovering over our faces as the door is slammed shut and the car speeds away from the sidewalk. Peering out of the window at a confused looking Johnny, he shoots forward in the BMW and instantly crashes into an oncoming vehicle that tactfully blocks his escape. My eyes flick around wildly, and it's then that I spot who is in the driver's seat. None other than my so-called mentor. Patrick.

The Beginning of the End

"What the hell?!" I scream, lifting my knees to my chin and shoving my boots into the back of the driver's seat. Patrick doesn't react, but his friend does.

"Hey! Behave or I'll give you a reason to," he snarls, grabbing the stuffed giraffe from my clutched fingers. Keeping the gun level with August's face, he bites down on the toy's ear and rips the head from its body in one easy move. My nostrils flare as he tosses my gift aside, the resemblance of his face coming back to me now. Dark stubble on his jaw, a tweed jacket clinging to his thick shoulders. He's the man from the alley that first night. The one who mistook me for someone else.

Dodging the traffic and blaring his horn, Patrick maneuvers the city like everyone else are puppets on his strings. He swerves to force vehicles aside, screams out the cracked blackened windows as he mounts the sidewalk. I suppose he's considerate enough to not leave a string of bodies trailing behind, but the hatred brimming under the surface of my skin won't be quelled. Patrick has gone too far this time.

"Whatever stupid lesson this is, in ambush tactics or whatever, isn't funny." I huff, crossing my arms. Patrick chuckles dryly, refusing to meet my angered gaze in the rear-view mirror. I don't care what he wants to do to me, knowing it's all in the name of my survival, but I refuse to let him drag August into it. Leaving the city behind, I peer back in the hopes that Johnny has managed to catch up, although I know it's pointless. No one could have followed Patrick's erratic driving, and as the city grows smaller and smaller, it's clear no one is following us. Sighing, I push my knee again August's, trying to reassure him with a small smile that everything will be okay. Obviously, with a gun shoved in his face, he's not inclined to agree.

Swerving onto a side road I didn't notice between the rows of trees, the car bumps heavily, tossing us around like a salad. We're the piece of limp lettuce in this analogy. Shadows close in as even the sun abandons us and we're left to the mercy of the moon. A slip of a crescent, barely strong enough to penetrate the trees overhead.

In no time, we're skidding to a stop outside a wooden cabin, and the man is ordering us to get out. Keeping August's fingers locked in mine, I pull his frozen frame out behind me.

"Hey, just like you kept me safe at the zoo, I'll keep you safe now. I know these people," I half lie. "They're a bit messed up, but everything will be fine." With my efforts to reassure him, August crawls out of the car and allows Tweed Jacket to shove us up the porch steps. Patrick unlocks the cabin door and heads inside first, rustling around out of sight. Stepping inside, I take the liberty of hitting the lights and look over our surroundings. There's no furniture, aside from a single chair in the centre of the room. Beneath it, a large dust sheet covers most of the wooden planks that mirror the cladding on the inside walls.

"What are we supposed—" I start, when Patrick dives out from behind the door to attack August with a thickly corded rope. I shout and try to pry his hands free, digging my nails deeply into Patrick's flesh, but he doesn't care. With the help of his friend, the pair nudge me aside and bind August's arms to his body, tightly enough to cut his skin. Even more worryingly is how August doesn't shout or try to defend himself. He just accepts being shoved towards the seat in the centre of the room.

Patrick pushes down on his shoulders and August obeys, holding my eye while the men tie his ankles and wrists to the chair.

"What are you doing?" I whisper, the instant the men step back, not stopping me when I run to his side. Large, haunted hazel eyes slide my way, not a trace of mirth left on August's impassive face.

"Hostage training. Don't fight back or they'll see it as a challenge," he mutters. Dipping his head, August's lips brush my ear and I close my eyes briefly, trying to steal some of his strength.

"That's enough," Patrick says, kicking me aside so I'm not near August anymore. Toppling onto my back, Patrick steps half over me and lowers to stroke one of his fingers in the fraying gloves over my face.

"We really could have had something, you know." He breathes, and I tense up. "Give it a few years, and you'll be one hell of a feisty woman. Possibly the most talented pickpocket around, thanks to me. We could have ruled this city." When his face lingers close enough for his foul breath to wash over me, I resist gagging in favor of throwing my head forward to catch him off guard. Unfortunately, Patrick is faster than me and he grips onto my neck, using the hold to drag me back up to my feet.

"Do you feel like telling me what this is all about now?" I spit, the instant he releases me, my tone laced with venom. August doesn't deserve to be dragged into the drama Patrick seems to emit, so the sooner this is over with, the better.

Patrick's friend appears again, entering the cabin with my backpack in his hand. Slamming the door closed, he draws the length of my baseball bat free of the bag and tosses it across the floor to land at my feet.

"I didn't put all the pieces together at first," Patrick muses, pacing back and forth as if retelling his favorite story. "But, Sal here, never misses a trick. We were sitting on a gold mine this entire time, and had no idea."

"My family has a specialist detective company on speed dial. They'll be here long before you manage to squeeze a ransom out of them," August jerks his head up in defiance. Naively, it's only at that moment I realize this isn't a game. Or a test. Or a lesson. Patrick is serious. His friend, Sal, laughs to himself like a nutcase, the gun in his hand shaking all over the place.

"Not you," he sneers at August. Then his all-knowing eyes settle on me. "Her." I frown, jerking back as if I've been psychically slapped.

"Me? I have nothing. I'm no one."

"Give it up, little one," Patrick growls, running a gloved hand over his tattered beanie. "We know the truth. Why do you think people have been chasing you all over the city since you turned up?"

"But...those men. You stopped them from hurting me. You—"

"Had already accepted your bounty," Patrick grins widely. "I'm about to become a very wealthy man, and all those on the street can kiss my ass if they think I'll remember them when I am." The pieces begin to slot together in my mind, although the information is too much to bear. He sold me out, to some anonymous source who is paying for my delivery. Or maybe… my return. My foster dad, it has to be. No one else would know or care about me enough to part with their hard earned cash. My foster dad is probably desperate to get me back under his firm rule, to lock me away where no one would ever hear my screams again.

"Patrick, no." I shake my head, dropping to my knees. "Please, don't do this. Don't send me back."

"Too late. A designated collector is already on his way to pick you up. But while we're waiting, I thought we'd have a little fun." His eyes dance with delight while mine are utterly confused. Smoothing my hands down my leggings, I try to get a grip of myself and focus on my survival, rather than fall victim to my own demons. Swooping down onto one knee, Patrick tilts his head as if I'm dense.

"You know, if you'd shown me some kind of loyalty, I might have decided against turning you in. But you ditched me every chance you got, to hang out with him." Patrick glares at August with unhidden distaste. Lifting the bat, he pushes the wood into my hands and lifts me by my arms. "You've been getting too attached. It's for your own good if you break off whatever is happening here before you go. Odds are, you won't be returning." Taking a step back, I stand there, frowning at the bat in my hands.

"I don't…understand," I say, although I think I do. I just refuse to do it.

"Break your attachment to him. Break *him*. It'll be good for you." Patrick grins. Sal bobs up and down, any resemblance of a man with his shit together is long gone. He's a straight up psychopath with a deadly weapon in his hand. Not a good mix.

"No." I shake my head. "I'm not going to hurt August. He's my..."

"Boyfriend," Sal mocks in a sissy voice. As if that's the most ridiculous notion in the world. That someone like August would fall for a girl like me. Trying to toss the bat aside, Patrick is there in an instant, gripping my hands around the wood.

"Hit. Him," he grits out, and I continue to shake my head. "Hit him!" he bellows right in my face, and again, I refuse. "I swear, Candy, if you don't hit him, I will, and it'll be twice as hard." I bear my teeth, full out snarling at Patrick's threat, but still, I fight to shift my hands off the bat.

"You're insane." I shove my weight into Patrick's chest. When that does nothing, I spit in his face. Quick as a flash, he jolts the bat aside and it smacks me in the jaw. Pain blossoms there, but nothing I can't handle.

"Just do it." August's voice breaks through the curtain of red flooding my vision. Sitting so still, his defeated hazel eyes plead with me to do as Patrick says. "It's okay, I know it's not you."

"No! I'm not going to hit you! Not if I'm being told to, or even if I wanted to. I lo—" The flash of headlights brightens the room, a vehicle pulling up outside the filthy windows. Sighing, Patrick pushes me away with a shove and I step up to August's side. Taking the chance, because I might not get another, I lean down and press a hard kiss on August's mouth while Patrick's back is turned. I don't know if it manages to convey all of my feelings in that one touch of our lips, but the quiver to his says it does. He hears me loud and clear.

"Oh well, looks like your ride is here." Patrick directs my attention back towards the window. "Sal, finish this." Patrick flicks his wrist back in our general direction while heading for the door. My eyes barely shift to Sal's menacing ones as the crack of the gun ricochets through the cabin. I flinch and scream on instinct, touching my torso for signs of a hole, but there is none.

Huffing out a sigh of relief that Sal is as rubbish a shot as he looks, August's head knocks against my hip and I reach out for his hair on instinct. Except he doesn't react. In fact, his head rolls further back, as if he's not in control of it, or he's...

"August?" I frown. Stepping aside, I peer down, my brain not catching up with the siren blaring in my head. A singular bullet hole has penetrated August's sheer white t-shirt, the red leaking behind it almost too cartoon-like to be real. Nudging my foot against his, I kick him once, twice, and then harder in the shin. "Stop messing around. You're scaring me," I tell him, but there's no response. There's just...nothing.

Dropping the bat, I kneel between his legs and place a hand over the redness marring his shirt. My hand comes away warm and sticky, and I repeat the process with the other. Pulling his head forward to face me, the redness on my hands stains his jaw line as I give him a shake. I don't understand. He was talking to me mere moments ago, offering to take a beating from me, and now he's not there. The bubbly mirth in his features gone, his unblinking hazel eyes vacant.

"August? August!" My voice splutters out in breathy huffs. My lungs constrict, choking me from the inside. Blackness coats my vision, followed by white dots that blur the scene before me. All the while, Sal's cackling howls can be heard. The more I suffer, the harder he laughs. Yet, I can't believe what my head is telling me. Not this sweet, kind, generous boy. He has so much to live for, so much to achieve. It should be me. "Au...Au...gus," I begin to weep.

"Actually," a gruff voice sounds, so loud I could swear it was directly inside my own head. "It's An-gus, if you don't mind," Dropping the head clutched between my hands so it lolls back on lifeless shoulders, I blink rapidly to clear my vision.

At first I thought my hair was covering part of my face, but no, there's a smudge of pink sitting on August's knee. Rubbing the bloody heels of my palms against my eyes, I finally make out the shape of a gummy bear, patiently waiting with an evil grin and a pair of tilted black eyebrows. "Well, hey there. Nice to see you've come around. What do you say we kill the chortling motherfucker behind you and save the formal introductions for later?"

"Kill him?" I ask. The gummy bear, Angus, nods his jiggly head, his smile growing.

"Kill the bastard."

"Kill the bastard," I echo numbly. Sitting back on my heels, I grab for my bat. Standing on hollow legs, I peer down at the body tied to the chair, my recent reaction fleeting. Like I could be watching a movie, I feel detached, as if my emotional switch has just been flicked to 'off'.

"Thank me for that later," Angus agrees with the notion, hoping down onto the ground. Procuring a pink bat of his own, I follow his waddled steps towards Sal, where he shows me how to swing. "Like this." Angus swipes the bat across Sal's shins. Stepping up behind him, Sal is busy wiping the tears from his eyes when I mimic the gummy bear. Crack.

Shouting in shock, Sal's head whips to mine, and Angus yells my next instruction. Smacking the gun from his hand, it skids across the ground while I bring the bat down hard on Sal's face. A few teeth go flying, and before he can react, I hit him again. This time in the head, and he topples over like a Jenga tower. I suppose I've found my sweet spot. Reeling the bat back, I stick to that area of Sal's scalp. Beating and battering.

Pounding and pummelling, until the pink end of my bat is marred with the brain matter of a halfwit who's laughed his last laugh.

My chest is heaving, my breaths short, as I throw down the bat one last time on a scream, splintering it in half across Sal's unrecognizable face. Leaving it there, I vow to replace my weapon of choice with a bigger and better version, one with a cool name and spongier grip.

Hunting around for Angus, I find him in a mini sun lounger by the tossed gun, his eyes peering at me over a pair of sunglasses.

"Very nicely done. Time to get out of here?" he asks. Striding over, I scoop up the gun and turn to head towards the door. The boy in the chair has my footsteps halting, my gaze searching his face one last time. Dragging my hand over his face, I close his ghostly hazel eyes, muttering beneath my breath.

"It may not seem like it right now, but you're one of the lucky ones." Without wasting another moment, I walk over to the doorway. It's cracked open ever so slightly, and I flick the light switch, plunging myself into darkness. Without my shadow to give me away, I peer through the gap and spot my targets. A man in black fatigues, casually smoking a cigarette, and with his back to me, Patrick.

"Fucking Patrick," Angus growls, and I grunt in agreement. Raising the gun, I exhale slowly through my nose and close one eye. "Both eyes open," Angus tells me, perching himself on my shoulder. Nodding, I try again, setting my sights on the fraying beanie clinging to Patrick's head. Bang. Bye bye, asshole.

I don't know what surprises me more, the accuracy of my aim, or the way I handle the blowback of the pistol. Who said shooting games are detrimental to teenagers? The guy puffing on his cigarette panics, reaching for a gun of his own, but I'm faster. Sending a bullet on its merry journey to his chest, I yank the door open and trot down the steps with my new companion.

"Wait," the dirty smoker rasps, as I step over him. "I have…information…you want-"

"Oh yeah? I've got some handy info too. One in four people die of lung cancer. Congrats, you just beat the odds." Planting a bullet between his eyes, I pry the keys from his pants pocket and help myself to his car. A new-plate Mercedes with a plush, black and silver interior.

Sliding into the driver's seat, I adjust the seat all the way forward and sag in the seat. I'm only going to take it a few miles down the road until I find a place to ditch and burn it, but for now, I'll revel in the smell of fresh leather. I should be thinking about what I'll do next. How I'll rid myself of the blood on my hands, where I'll go to find safety. But, none of that serious shit matters anymore. Life is momentary, but fun lasts forever.

"Nice one!" Angus applauds me from the passenger seat, and I give him a small bow. Revving up the engine, I peel out of the dirt track, grinning like Cruella on her way to skin some puppies. Except, my favorite flavor won't be Dalmatians, it'll be any bitch that tries to get in my way. I'm Candy Crystal; the one, the only. The original. If nothing else, at least I've learnt one fundamental life lesson tonight. A man will never best me again.

UNANSWERED QUESTIONS? KEEP READING!

Hello my lovelies! Maddison here (very briefly) to say thank you so much for reading the prequel in the I Love Candy Series. Someone as complex as Candy needed a backstory, and I'm so excited to bring this insight into the feisty, badass FMC we all love. All of those unanswered questions currently rattling around your noggin are waiting to be solved in the rest of the series!

The I Love Candy Series is a dark reverse harem romance, which is now officially complete! You can carry on bingeing through to the end, starting right now with a the first chapter of Crushin' Candy, book one, on the very next page! Grab some gummy bears and glitter-infused gin, and from the bottom of my heart, I hope you love Candy as much as I do. Bye for now.

CANDY

"Sup." I nod to the crackheads and hobos loitering across the cell benches. The metal grate slams shut behind me and I throw a wink back at Captain Knobstick. He became my main interrogator four arrests ago, and even though he can never make a charge stick, I feel like we've really bonded. The balding man is eye-line with me at 5′ 8″, with a wide gap between his front two teeth, and a dead caterpillar living on his upper lip.

Grimacing at me, he walks away whilst trailing his baton across all the bars. Music to my ears, I sigh to myself. Digging out the piece of gum wedged between my back teeth and cheek, I cross the space and pop a bubble at the gangly girl quivering in the corner.

"You're in my seat." She actually flinches, her dull hair shaking around her ankles, since her knees are pulled up to her chest. I wait a whole ten seconds before growling to make her shift aside, taking my favorite spot. Turning away from the others, I lie back on the bench and lift my PVC-covered legs to lean them against the wall. There's a small whimper from the girl, and if she starts to cry, I'll be putting her out of her misery. Only with a mild concussion, but everyone would thank me for it. Except, maybe her.

"First time, huh?" I blow a large pink bubble before popping it. I think she nods amongst her trembling, her wide doe eyes swinging to me like a gazelle spotting a lioness. Well, rawr to you too.

"Y-y-yeah, but it wasn't my fault! I swear! I was just trying to finish my college essay at the Starbucks on Vine Street, before the deadline, when a masked person barreled straight into the table. My coffee spilled all over my laptop and I was so worried about my essay, I didn't even notice the drugs that had been stashed in my bag until the police dogs caught up to me."

Twisting my head properly to the side, I lift my hands in circles to hold them over my eyes and squint. My mask often rides up during a healthy jog from the cops, and I'll be damned, it is her.

Giggles slip through my chewing until I'm in full hysterics, on my back once more. What are the chances my ignorant partner-in-crime would be in the same holding cell as me? I ran for fucking miles. Cardio has always been my best friend though, along with strawberry milkshakes, donuts, rainbow sprinkles, and a load of bullshit other reasons I need to keep cardio on my good side.

The smile is hurting my cheeks, until I suddenly realize what else her presence means, and the laughter dies. An abrupt and painful death. I go slack and impossibly still on the bench, with my eyes stare at a spot on the ceiling. Fuck, that means my plan to stalk her and break into her student dorms at some point tomorrow to retrieve my stash is royally fucked. Instead, it's living the life with its illegal friends in an evidence locker beneath my feet somewhere. Big Chuuuu is not going to like this.

"Oh well," I say, making my neighbor flinch again. I'll blame Gangly Girl for not knowing better, and he'll just add it to my lifetime worth of debt. Running his errands is all I have to live for anyway, so I might as well keep them coming.

Even the thrill of being arrested has lost its appeal. No matter what tactics I use, being interrogated just doesn't fill my veins with the same sense of adrenaline. What does it take for them to pull out the big guns? Call the secret service, waterboard me, attach electrocution clamps to my nipples, or something?! I reckon I'll have to find a way to pay for it myself at this rate, but I already know I'm too much of a Dom to let a man completely overpower me.

"I've missed the deadline now," a soft voice sounds. Despite thinking about her, I'd forgotten my accomplice was still sitting next to me. She tucks her head into her knees and begins to sob. Rolling my eyes, I lean over and flick her in the temple.

"Don't they teach you anything useful at that college of yours? Police dogs are trained to scent fear, not drugs. You must have had something to hide or you wouldn't be here." This catches her off guard, her glazed-over brown eyes looking to the others for how to respond. Good luck with that one. This lot are too high or dejected to care.

"He seems rather focused on you," a gruff voice sounds inside my head. I twist to look at Angus on the bench above my head, his eyeless sockets focused on a guy across the other side of the cell. On second look, he does seem to be staring. Heavy dreads sit upon his youngish face, his smooth, chocolate skin and dark eyes are something I would usually be all over, if it weren't for his fixed scowl.

"Apparently so," I agree. "Can't blame him though." I blow a kiss to get some sort of reaction. Nothing. When I can't peg where I slightly recognize him from, I tuck my hands behind my head and return to looking at the ceiling, when Gangly Girl braves speaking to me again.

"W-who are you talking to?"

"Angus." I tut. The little fucker hops his way over my face and sits on my chest, a cringe worthy noise sounding with each moment. Like leather being stretched. *Shudder*. Noticing the girl's large eyes are still focused on me, and waiting for more, I sigh. "He's the pink gummy bear that follows me around and fills my head with his terrible wisdom. Like a mascot, who always leads me wrong, or the little squishy devil on my shoulder." I leave out the part about him having the voice of a chain-smoker, or how he curses like a blind seamstress.

"Why's he called Angus?" her small voice asks. I lean forward up on my forearms at this, briefly swiping one arm to knock the little shit to the floor. No one's ever asked me that before. Usually I get shrink referrals, or avoided completely, which is what I was hoping for, but now I'm intrigued.

"Because he's pink, spews shit, and puts the 'G' in anus." I smirk, remembering how clever thirteen-year-old me thought I was coming up with that when he first appeared. Gangly Girl nods to herself, not seeming too bothered by me as she looks away. On second thought, I reckon she's feeling so lost in pity and despair, nothing else matters. I know that feeling. Maybe if life hadn't fucked me anally with a dirty stick, I might have been like her. Innocent, rigid, boring.

Nah, fuck that. I'll take all the shit to be me. I'm Candy fucking Crystal—not my legal middle name, but the rest is authentic. My mother was a stripper before one too many years of drugs took its toll on her, and I was the product of one of her clients. No idea who, and I couldn't care less. She'd never wanted to be a mom, but after the legal system and dozens of group homes raised me, she thought I'd run into her arms and plead to join the family business. No thank you. I love my body, from my cute set of abs to my long legs. My neon pink hair hangs just past my shoulders, my left arm and chest inked with exaggerated caricatures of superheroes. But they belong to me. Not someone's lying husband in a seedy club. Mine.

Anyways, where was I? Oh yeah. Swinging my legs around, I take pity on the girl I've decided is my protégé.

"Here." I pull my gum in half with my teeth. "Chew this." When she doesn't immediately open, I lunge forward and pry her mouth open, not without gaining some teeth marks on my fingers though. Feisty, I love it. Popping the gum into her mouth, I clamp her jaw shut and give her my best death stare until she begins to chew.

"Good girl." I pat her on the head. Next, my eyes fall to her top. It's navy and fits nicely, except for the excess lace covering the top of her bust, up to her neck. What is this girl, a nun? Expecting her to put up a fight, I swing myself around to straddle her, trapping her arms by her side with my thighs. Ripping the top half off, she bucks and shrieks, but it's no use. Master Splinter taught me everything he knew whilst I was growing up, and the library let me stay late to watch Teenage Mutant Ninja Turtles on a weekend. It beat going back to the group home, and I gave those bookcases a run for their money.

The metal grate slides open, Captain Knobstick shouting my name along with the satisfying sound of a taser. Oh yeah, it's on.

"Candy, you're free to go. Don't make me use this on you." I give my apprentice one last look over and smirk, happy with my work. Rising from her lap, I slowly spin to face the clammy officer opposite.

"How about you give me one spark for the road, and I

promise not to be back for at least...a month?" Angus sucks in a croaky breath. I know, mate. Big words, but if that's what it takes, I'll do my best to stick to it. Knobstick is slowly shaking his head, and the way he's pursing his lips makes the caterpillar dance. Maybe I'm wrong, it might be a hairy worm instead.

Hanging my head low, I walk by defeatedly and wait for the grate to be closed. I lean mournfully on the other side, bidding my student goodbye, with the promise I'll find her to finish what I started. Her eyes nearly pop out of her head, and I then realize the threat that could be inferred in my words. To ease her mind, I blow her a kiss, but somehow, I think I've had the opposite effect. Knobstick nudges me along, my eyes locking with the guy who is still staring at me with every step I take. There's a few dreads cut short at the back of his head and it suddenly comes to me.

"Dude!" I grip my side as laughter roars out of me, my finger pointing at him through the bars. I remember now! There was a downtown scavenger hunt last year, and a handful of his dreads declared me Scumbag of the Year. I got a mini trophy and an ounce of weed, it was an awesome day. Sure, I probably should have asked him first, but he was being wheeled into an ambulance to have his stomach pumped at the time. It's not my fault he can't handle his poison of choice, or that the paramedics are so easily distracted by their vehicle having a bitch fit. Whether I tampered with the wires or not was neither here nor there—I won something for the first time in my life!

Knobstick throws me back just as the guy collides with the other side of the bars, the tears streaming from my eyes making my reactions slow. Making my way into the stairwell, leading back up to the precinct, I can't hold back the streams of laughter that echo around the walls. I needed that pick me up.

The station is mostly deserted, since it's stupid o'clock in the morning. I'm escorted all the way to the front desk, a large-set woman sitting on the other side of the glass eyeing me closely. I briefly wonder why bother with the red lipstick, since her uniform is crinkled and her greasy hair is in a messy bun that I reckon she's slept in for a few days, until I see her expression soften at Captain Knobstick. I raise an eyebrow, noticing the shy blush entering his cheeks, until the wedding band on his finger catches my attention.

My hand twitches, the taser on his belt so close, and Angus egging me on in my head to do it. Teach this cheater a lesson. Jab him right in the sternum and let the volts shock the deceit right out of him. Short-circuit his heart. Hide his lifeless body in the back of a bin truck. Wait, what? Shut the fuck up, Angus. I'm inside a police station, for fuck's sake.

Willing my hand to relax, I return my attention to the adulteress on the other side of the glass. I can't ignore the small rush of adrenaline I briefly felt however, like the kiss of an old acquaintance in all the right places. A leather jacket and a brown envelope is dumped on the counter before me, my name scribbled across the front messily. Without moving an inch, I maintain eye contact with her.

"Where's my bat?"

"We can't return potential weapons to those who have been in our custody," she drawls. I squint slightly, fully prepared to not only take down Knobstick but every fucker in this place if I a) I don't get my bat back in the next five seconds, and b) if so help me, there happens to be a scratch on it.

A chill shudders through my spine, my breathing hard to keep controlled. There's a time and a place to utterly lose one's shit, and this isn't it. Instead, I pull on all of my reserves to speak low and calmly.

"I've been in your custody long enough to know there's a

photo of a pretty blonde and twin girls on his desk." I jerk my chin to the officer tensing beside me. "And unless you've reallllllllly let yourself go and had a full facial reconstruction, it's not you. How about you fetch my bat, and I won't start screaming the word affair on repeat until your ears bleed?" All of the color in her face drains, but she doesn't move straight away. Shrugging, I tuck away my gum and open my mouth wide on an inhale. "AF—"

"Okay! Okay, fine," she hisses. Reaching beneath her desk, she produces my beloved bat with barely any effort at all. I smile sweetly, smoothing my hand over every memorized crevice in the wood.

"See, that wasn't so hard." Grabbing the brown envelope, I spin and leave with a backwards wave. I'll be back before they get too comfortable.

It's pitch black outside, not a single star shining down on New York City tonight. Thankfully, it's the height of summer, so the air is balmy enough to not need to put my jacket on as I skip down the stone steps. I'm not too far from my current place of residence, but I hail a taxi anyway, not wanting to get myself in more trouble walking around with my bat in my hand in the dead of night.

Dropping into the back seat, I lean over to strap Angus in before taking my phone out of the envelope and switching it on. The home screen has barely loaded when it starts to vibrate with the incoming of a stream of messages. All from the Big Cheese, and all coded, of course.

Big Cheese: Where are you? Dinner has gone cold. (AKA, the warehouse I was stealing the haul from is now empty.)

Big Cheese: Found you. Mom was worried sick. (AKA, I know you're in jail, again.)

Big Cheese: Don't forget your cousins are in town, I'll send a car round to pick you up so you aren't late tomorrow night as well. (AKA, my presence is required at the mansion, and there will be an audience for my public spanking.)

"Dammit!" I slam my hand into the passenger head rest, causing the driver to skid to a stop and send me flying forward. Shit, should have worn my seatbelt. Muttering an apology, I settle back and toss my phone into the seat beside me.

Pulling up a little further down my street—because letting others know your address is a rookie mistake—I hop out and hold the door open long enough to let Angus squelch his way out.

"Hey, that's $21!" the cabby shouts at me through the window when I go to walk away. "Night's rates!" I look over my shoulder, my worldly possessions huddled in my arms.

"You really should have checked that I had money before accepting me as a rider. " I shrug. Walking away, he makes a fuss of cussing and beeping his horn before speeding away. Wow, road-rage much.

Closing in on my place, a minibeast crosses my path and hisses at me. I scowl at Sphinx, my landlady's little shit of a hairless Egyptian cat. He's missing one eye, and is all wrinkly like foreskin, but I do appreciate his 'stroke me or die' attitude. Scooping him up by the collar, he makes a screeching noise until I dump him in my leather jacket and start to scratch his tummy. Prickly on the outside, pussy on the inside—I get that.

I make it to the main building, shoving Sphinx into the cat flap before taking the hidden steps around the side down to the basement level. My keys are in the envelope, with a fluffy pink pom-pom and little plastic gummy bear attached. I smirk at Angus who has jumped up onto my shoulder, juggling my bat as I unlock the door.

"Home sweet home." I breathe in the scent of damp as I step inside.

"Shithole, sweet shithole more like," Angus adds unhelpfully. The lightbulb flickers overhead when I switch it on, so I just leave it off. Dumping everything on the plastic table in the centre of the living room/kitchen/dinner combo, the weight of the day suddenly falls over me. My skin-tight leggings and corset go next, the air wrapping my body in a welcoming embrace. Grabbing the handle on the wall, I tug my fold away bed down onto its squeaking metal legs and drop onto the thin mattress.

"Good night, shitface," I mutter into the material, intending it for Angus. Sleep has just begun to claim me when his reply filters in, a small smile pulling at the corner of my mouth.

"Sweet dreams, fucktard."

ACKNOWLEDGMENTS

Thank you so much to each and every one of you for taking a chance on the I Love Candy series. You have taken to my foul-mouthed, murder-hungry psycho like a pig in mud, and I'm very grateful. I promise you the series just keeps getting better and better, so make sure you binge them all now.

This series wouldn't be as amazing as it is without the help of some fantastic people.

TO AMY - This series and this prequel wouldn't have been completed if it wasn't for you. You have been a rock to me while I've been writing this, and your support has been invaluable. Thank you for loving Candy and her guys as much as I do.

TO SAM - I would be lost without you. You are such a lovely person, and you help keep my life organised. Thank you for all your help, support, and more importantly, your friendship.

TO JESSICA - Without your amazing creative mind, this story would never have happened. You created the covers that inspired me to write Candy. Without you, none of Candy's world would exist. Thank you for creating our favourite crazy psycho!

TO EMMA - As always, thank you for making the formatting of the book so good. I give you a slight idea, and you nail it every time. And this time you helped with the edits too. Thanks for being the best co-writer and friend!

TO MY FAMILY - Thank you for being so patient with me while I write. I know there are times when writing encroaches on family time, but you are always so supportive and never complain. Extra thanks to Mr Cole for supporting me even though I probably spend more time with my laptop than him some days. I love you all, and I'm so lucky to have such a supportive family.

TO YOU, THE READERS - thank you to each and every one of you for picking up my book and devouring the words. Your love for Candy and her guys means the world to me. I wouldn't be able to keep writing and producing more books without your continued support. I can't wait for you to see what I have lined up next!

ABOUT THE AUTHOR

Maddison is a married mum of two, and a serial daydreamer. As a huge fan of all romance troupes, from RH to Omegaverse, she finally decided to put pen to paper (finger to keyboard doesn't sound as poetic) and write her own.

As a child, life was moving around the UK and a short stint in the Caribbean, before Maddison has found herself back in the south east of England where she is now happily settled. With a double award in applied arts and an A-level in art history, Maddison is an average musical-loving, Disney-obsessed, jive-dancer with a dark passion for steamy fantasy books.

FOLLOW MADDISON COLE

If you're a new reader to me – welcome to the mad house! My list of writes can be found below and for up-to-date info, make sure to follow my socials! The readers group is the best place for reveals, announcements, giveaways and more, and please never hesitate to reach out! I love hearing from readers

Sign up to my newsletter here:
http://eepurl.com/hx3Zqr

Also, make sure to join my Facebook readers group, Cole's Reading Moles here:
www.facebook.com/colesreadingmoles

You can also find me on TikTok here:
https://www.tiktok.com/@coles_moles

ALSO BY MADDISON COLE

I LOVE CANDY
Dark Humor RH - Completed

Findin' Candy (novella)
https://amzn.to/3bcueOp

Crushin' Candy
https://amzn.to/3n0TASf

Smashin' Candy
https://amzn.to/3Oniuai

Friggin' Candy
https://amzn.to/3QwlmUb

.

ALL MY PRETTY PSYCHOS
Paranormal RH with ghosts and demons

Queen of Crazy
https://amzn.to/3O4biQt

Kings of Madness
https://amzn.to/3HzvBCY

Hoax: The Untold Story (pre-order)

https://amzn.to/3xAJhcA

Reign of Chaos (pre-order)
https://amzn.to/3b95PcI

.

THE WAR AT WAVERSEA
Basketball College MFM Menage - Completed

Perfectly Powerless
https://amzn.to/3OqHTQp

Handsomely Heartless
https://amzn.to/3tMoRfu

Beautifully Boundless
https://amzn.to/3MYiiNG

.

THE SHADOWED SOULS
New Adult Romantic Suspense - Completed

Devilishly Damaged
https://amzn.to/3bcuXz7

Deceitfully Damaged
https://amzn.to/3zOY6ei

Dangerously Damaged
https://amzn.to/3OtlqSD

MOON BOUND

Vampire/Shifters Fated Mates Standalones

Exiled Heir

https://amzn.to/3OtlqSD

Privileged Heir

https://amzn.to/3mYwQ5g

WILLOWMEAD ACADEMY (CO-WRITTEN WITH EMMA LUNA)

Sexy Student - Teacher Taboo Age Gap Standalone

Life Lessons

https://amzn.to/3tL8eAX

Printed in Great Britain
by Amazon